TALES
from the
BIKE SHOP

TALES
from the
BIKE SHOP

by *Maynard Hershon*

Illustrations by Jef Mallett

VITESSE PRESS
Brattleboro, Vt.

*To Owen Mulholland,
without whom there
would be no stories or book.*

*To Rich Carlson at Winning,
without whom lots of the stories
wouldn't read nearly so well.*

*To Grant Petersen,
without whom there might not
have been a book nearly so soon.*

*To bike riders I know
and will get to know,
without your friendship I might as well
not have bothered to pump my tires.*

ISBN 0-941950-24-7
Library of Congress card number 89-51267

Text design by Irving Perkins Associates
Cover illustration by Jef Mallett
Cover design by Optima Communications

Published by Vitesse Press
A division of FPL Corporation
P.O. Box 1886
Brattleboro, VT 05302

Manufactured in the United States of America

CONTENTS

WATSON'S BIKE

WE KNEW Don quite a while before he told us about Watson's bike. He first saw it, he said, for sale at a police auction back where he used to live. Right away he felt sure he'd found Watson's old bicycle, the green Harry Quinn Watson rode when he won all those races.

Every bike racer around here has heard about Watson. How he could hang on in a race even when his tongue dragged on his front tire. How he wasn't a natural at climbing but couldn't be left behind on a hill. How he could drag from some gritty place inside himself a finishing burst no one could touch.

In the legends, Watson looked on as cycling fads came and went. He watched as bike frames got longer or shorter and hubs went from high-flange to low and back again. He ignored it all and rode that Quinn.

Lots of racers without his class bought the latest French frames, Italian frames, or other English frames. They drilled their brake levers for lightness. They bought more and more expensive racing tires. Watson beat them on the flats. He beat them in the hills. He rode away almost at will.

Legend had it that burglars stole the bike after Watson quit racing. Years later, Don outbid an old man at the auction and took it home. He looked at it for hours, he told us, there in his room. He thought and thought about what it meant to own Watson's old bike.

Watson's bike rolled a little easier, climbed more eagerly...

The next day he unbolted the mismatched cheap equipment from Watson's frame and cleaned it thoroughly. The paint looked good. As far as Don could see, the insides of the tubes had never begun to rust. He took it to a shop to get it checked for alignment, and doggoned if it wasn't straight.

He told us he took the usable parts off his own bike and installed them on the Quinn. You could tell, listening to Don talk, that he'd been excited and anxious to ride it. He hoped a little of Watson might have stayed with it and might rub off on him.

He bought a few new parts and installed them. He found an old-fashioned leather saddle, like the one he'd heard Watson rode, and put it on. All along, he kept his feelings to himself. He said nothing to his friends about his hunch that it wasn't just any old bike he'd come into.

When Don did start riding it, he told us, his legs felt light. The bike rolled a little easier, climbed more eagerly, and went downhill more confidently than other bikes. He began to make his training buddies hurt, toying with them, then choosing his moment to ride away. He could make them suffer as long as he wanted.

As his confidence grew, he said, he became kinder to his riding friends. He sat in the pack on rides, doing only his share of the pacesetting. He stopped making things so tough for the rest of the guys. He did go all-out for sprints at city limit signs, and he would win even without drafting tactics—he was that fast. Riders looked up to him more and more.

Don's first race was a criterium in a town near here, a typical flat race around a long city block. He told us later he was nervous at the start, but I stood on the start/finish line and watched him hang in and win a midrace sprint for a prime prize. He finished third, his path to the line blocked by slower riders. The prime win seemed easy, he said. He couldn't wait to race again.

He entered a hilly road race with one especially steep climb. He and two other men broke away, leaving the pack a minute behind at the base of the hill. On the climb, the other two tried short testing bursts of speed. Don matched their efforts easily. The third time one of them jumped, Don responded by blasting past and dropping them both. He never looked back.

Don won race after race. His sense of the green bike's legacy grew steadily stronger. Sometimes he could feel energy coming off it in waves as it leaned against the wall in his room. During races he could sense it telling him he wasn't exhausted, that he had not spent it all, that there was more. When he believed and tried, there was more. He used it, and he won.

Still, he told us, he never could talk about the bike and its history. He knew the effort was his own. He knew he imagined any inspiration he felt from the machine, but his success did not satisfy him. His bike had made him, somehow, and he was a little ashamed.

By the time Don moved here to go to school, we all knew who he was. He dropped by Bob's shop once or twice to say hi while he was enrolling for classes. He had heard of Bob, as you'd imagine, so he hung around as his schedule allowed to try and listen in on a few of Bob's old-days stories.

The guys looked forward to riding with Don. We wanted to see if he was as fast as we'd heard sprinting for our city limit signs. And he was, every bit as fast. He beat us regularly, but he never acted like anything special. I didn't think he got much of a kick out of it at all.

Sure enough, as we talked about Don more and more at Bob's, Bob got a little curious himself. He joined us on a Wednesday morning training ride and fell in line next to Don. We warmed up in a double line out around the reservoir. I sat behind the two of them, listening in. Don would ask questions, and Bob would answer. Mostly Bob answered in a few words, but occasionally he'd warm to his subject.

At one point I heard Bob say he'd noticed Don's old Quinn. I saw Don's head turn. He looked intently at Bob as Bob said that old Watson rode a Quinn, too. Watson's, Bob said, was a lighter color green and was, of course, about two inches smaller. Watson, Bob explained, was only about five-three.

I was just able to see Don's face. He began to smile and then to laugh. I was puzzled. So was Bob. We both looked at him in wonder.

Then I spotted the Fairfield town limit. I saw Bob jump, out of the saddle, hard as he could for the sign. He sprinted smooth, spinning up a medium gear, but so fast I couldn't hang on in his draft. As I lost Bob's wheel I saw Don, going very fast, jump up to Bob for an instant, then come around, edging Bob at the sign, laughing, still laughing.

BUNNY HOP

MY WIFE and I put my bike in the car last September and drove down to the Central Coast area of California. We visited with her folks and spent a night or two in bed and breakfast inns in places like Ojai and Santa Barbara—neat places, especially for people who like to ride around on bicycles.

In Ojai I learned about a regular training ride in nearby Ventura Sunday mornings. I got up early, and off I drove, my bike on the roofrack. I found the place that'd been described to me as the start; there was no one there. A passing cyclist told me he knew of a ride starting across town, at a bike shop, and told me generally how to get there. After getting lost twice, at the last minute I pulled into the shopping center lot where the ride began.

There were more people unloading bikes there than I'd ever seen for a training ride. I thought, "Wow, these Ventura folks really turn out on a Sunday." I said hi to the guys in the car next to mine; they checked out my bike, making sure it met a minimum standard, before saying hi back. I noticed that people, oddly, seemed to be pulling out of the lot in small groups. When I asked about that, the guys said it would all sort out down the road. I nodded as if I understood.

I jumped into a likely-looking group of about 15 people, two or three women and guys from about 20 to 40 years old. Right away I liked the pace and the almost flat terrain. You could use the big chainring nearly all the time—not the case, bruddah, where I live. You could sit in the saddle and pedal in, say, the 52 × 17 I liked it.

About 15 miles out of Ventura, I asked the guy next to me in the paceline how far these rides usually went. I'd had in mind around 30 or 40 miles. After a moment of confusion, he told me that I had connected with an event called the Bunny Hop Century. Our group, he said, was headed for downtown Santa Barbara and back, about, as I remember, 72 miles.

I thought, "Hey, I can ride 72 miles," especially in the big ring at 20-plus mph. Also, I thought, "I don't believe I can find my way back to the start by myself." So it was Santa Barbara or bust with the hard-riding Mystery Cycling Club, of Deleted, California. Makes you tired just thinking about it, doesn't it? Does me.

As we motored up the coast highway, one of the women in our group got dropped and drifted back quite a bit, riding alone. Because I am such a super human being and a road cycling powerhouse, I dropped back and chatted with her for a while, then offered to tow her up to the group. "I can't keep up," Susan said. "Let's give it a try," I asserted positively.

She sat on my wheel, and I brought her back to her double-pacelined clubmates. After a few miles we came to what is called a hill in that area but might be called a rise or roller elsewhere. Again she lost a few feet and the help of the draft. I watched over my shoulder as she slowed and began to struggle. Inevitably, without the draft, the gap in front of her grew rapidly.

Once again, I dropped back, telling her she *could* hang in, that she was, in fact, only a *little* weaker, that we'd bridge again and she *could* hang on. She'd see, I said, that all she needed was to pick a smooth wheel to sit on, and she could stick. "No, *you'll* see," she told me. "I *had* a smooth wheel." I towed her up again anyway, watched her merge into the back of the group, and rode up to the front.

One guy up there, whose name is *not* Steve, really it's not, seemed to me to be the unofficial ride leader. He spent lots of time at the front and had a watchful, serious way. He looked like a bike rider. I said to him, "Steve *not* his real name, Susan can almost hang on. If we could hesitate just a second at the tops of the rises, she could ride the whole way with the group."

"She's a big girl," Steve said. "She can take care of herself." I admitted (weak, weak) that that was one way to look at it. I went to the back and thought about our little exchange. Certainly it was their club and their ride and none of my business. Certainly they had evolved their way of dealing with slower people over years of group rides.

Still, I didn't like what I felt was the coldness of it. I'd known groups like that before. They felt that if new people wanted badly enough to ride with them, they'd do what they had to so they could. If the new riders didn't (or couldn't) get fit enough, it was good riddance anyway. I told Susan, who had just gotten sawed off again, that I'd asked the gentleman in front, the one up there with the red helmet, if the group could just wait the least little bit. I told her what his answer had been.

She said that's just what she would've expected. She said she'd ridden with that same club for years. Some years she'd gotten really fit and couldn't be dropped. Other years, like this one, she couldn't quite hang on. They'd see her when she reached wherever they were headed. She knew of other, slower, friendlier clubs in her area, she said, but she liked this one, even when she couldn't keep up.

She said that when she first rode with them the effort of trying to hang on just one landmark farther made her fast. At that time, the club had not been friendly to women riders; she'd had to prove she could be fast enough and safe enough to qualify. Eventually they accepted her. It was clear to me that, even that September day when no one would wait for her, Susan felt proud of that acceptance.

Susan prized Steve's friendship and defended him valiantly when I told her about his "big girl" remark. She said that all along he's been the enforcer of the "no favors" code the club practices. After a long period of not being impressed by him, now she wouldn't change anything about the guy.

"What a tough woman," I thought. I don't believe that way of initiating new riders would work with me, were I to start all over again. Nothing encourages me more than a little success. Showing up weekend after weekend only to lack the horsepower or pack-savvy to survive the crunches in the group would get me down. I'd like to think I'd sense how neat it'd be to be one of the boys, so to speak, and keep on trying, but I bet I'd weaken. I know I'd give up long before Susan apparently did.

Clearly, the way Steve and the Mystery Cycling Club dealt with new riders worked great for Susan, as she will tell the world. Strong folks like Susan will persevere, enduring mini-failure after mini-failure until, ultimately, they triumph.

Also clearly, some folks are more easily dismayed than Susan—myself for instance. Still, folks like me might learn to survive just as well as she did. They might be just as proud of their progress as Susan is, just as protective of their leaders, if given an occasional few seconds of patient encouragement. Ride leaders should find plenty of opportunity to provide such encouragement, right at the tops of the hills.

DESPERATE MEASURES

PHIL STARTED getting terrible headaches. He hurt so bad he could hardly ride his bike. He had no appetite, and he snapped at people often. His friends quit calling. He took lots of aspirin and tried every remedy suggested to him. Nothing worked.

Doctor after doctor tried and failed to cure Phil. He kept riding his bike, shorter and shorter distances; the awful headaches made it hard to concentrate on the road. Soon he had to give up the bike. Phil decided then that the time had come for desperate measures.

He flew to a world-famous clinic in the Midwest and checked in for an exhaustive examination. Several renowned surgeons spent expensive hours with him in small, clean rooms. After two days there, he sat in a joyless gray cubicle, waiting. A young but serious physician brought the news.

"Phil," the doctor said, "the staff here has decided unanimously that your problem is testicular in origin. We urge you to consider surgical removal. I know, Phil, that you are a young and active man; this action may seem awfully final. We believe you will find that, given proper therapy and medication, you will be able to lead quite a normal, satisfying life."

Phil told the doctor he would have to think about it. He said he would be in touch within a week with an answer. Heavy-hearted, he flew home.

Phil tried to resume his life. He began daily short rides on his bike. Immediately he found he couldn't cope with his pain. He failed to speak kindly to his mom, with whom he lived, or his friends. Worst of all, he soon couldn't ride his bike.

Phil felt his life was scarcely worth living in such constant pain. He'd been home only eight days when he called the clinic and scheduled his surgery.

After the operation and a short period of bed rest, Phil flew home, the headaches completely gone. He found he had deep misgivings and remorse. Some days he would only sit and stare out a window at the beautiful late-spring countryside. His bike hung neglected in the garage, a cobweb forming in the spokes of the front wheel.

The May issue of his cycling club newsletter arrived. Phil read in it that his old hero, a famous Italian coach and *directeur sportif*, was to visit the town. The club had invited the old man, usually photo-graphed hugging a classic winner or emerging from the roof of some team car, to a special dinner in his honor. The newsletter said the old man had accepted.

Phil knew that opportunities to meet legends like this old man were rare. As he reread the newsletter, his phone rang. The club president called, saying the officers had taken it upon themselves to schedule a private appointment for Phil with the Italian coach and his inter-preter—as a kind of get-well gesture, the president said. They'd hoped Phil might become inspired to get back on his bike.

The club president told Phil to bring his bike to the meeting. The great man had offered to set Phil up on it, Italian pro-style, suggesting saddle height, stem length, and so on.

Phil said he was grateful for his old buddies' consideration. He agreed, somewhat reluctantly, to attend the dinner meeting and his audience with the fabled visitor. He took his bike down and pumped the tires, but he did not ride it until the evening of the event.

He pedaled to the restaurant, sat down, and ate his dinner with his bikie friends. He couldn't hear a word spoken by the guest of honor or the interpreter. Phil could feel the man's presence in the room, though. An unmistakable aura of authenticity surrounded the stocky gentleman. Here, indeed, sat the real thing. Phil began to get excited about his interview.

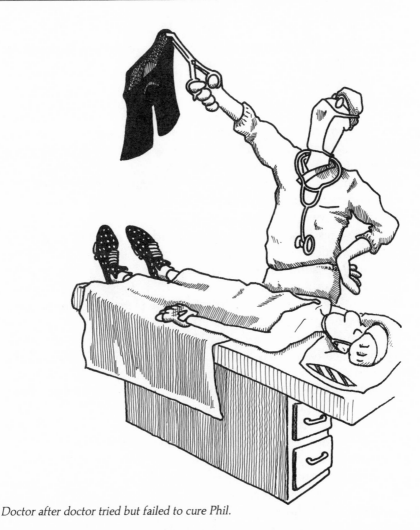

Doctor after doctor tried but failed to cure Phil.

The three men met in an adjacent room. Phil leaned his bike against a wall. He turned to face the interpreter and the man who had been the confidant of three decades of cycling superheroes. Phil asked the interpreter to express his respect for the old man and his delight at meeting him and enjoying his undivided attention.

Words were exchanged in soft Italian. The interpreter asked Phil if he would walk a little, back and forth, in the room. The coach watched Phil take a few tentative steps and then had Phil sit on his bike. He spoke through his translator.

"You are good climber?" the coach asked.

"I was, I guess," said Phil.

"The bicycle, it is one and one-half centimeters too small. And one centimeter too short in the horizontal tube," the interpreter translated. "Like Darrigade, when he started. You know Darrigade?"

Phil nodded yes, he'd heard of Darrigade.

"The stem should be 11 centimeters," said the interpreter, "with the shorter horizontal tube. And the saddle, the master says, should be higher, perhaps two centimeters higher."

Phil shook his head, amazed. How could the man know all these things? He needed no tape measure, no plumb line. He hadn't even asked Phil to pedal the bike. Phil was astonished.

"You have trouble with the knee, the left knee," the interpreter continued. "The toeclip is too short; the shoe-plate angled inward too acutely. Magni, yes Magni, too, had the same."

Phil's unbelief turned to awe. Hardly anyone knew about his occasional knee pain. "How can he know these things?" he asked the interpreter. As the question was relayed, the two Italians laughed.

"He is the greatest *directeur sportif*: the maestro, for 30 years," the answer came. Phil nodded, not knowing what to say.

"You wear the size 42 shoe, yes? Buy the 41 and soak it in water the first three rides. The 42 is too large," the interpreter continued.

"You wear the wool vest under the jersey, yes? And the size three Vittori Gianni shorts?"

Phil said no, he wore Sergal shorts, size two.

"No, no," said the interpreter, "you wear the size three Giannis."

"No, sir," Phil explained, "you got it all right but that. I wear size two Sergal shorts."

"No, you must wear the size three Giannis," translated the interpreter, "like Bartali. Bartali, he, also, wore the size two Sergal short instead of the size three Gianni. Pinched his balls. Gave him terrible headaches."

ALLIS

ALTOGETHER, THERE were about 10 of us new riders, juniors trying not to fall off and Cat IVs dreaming of making Cat III. We'd ride in the mornings, then we'd hang around Bob's shop in the afternoons. We liked to watch him fix bikes, and we'd encourage him to tell stories.

Bob never hid the fact that he held us guys in low regard, more or less. He did mention riders of the recent past who, he'd say, had earned his respect. Strong men, *they* were, riding hard on primitive, demanding bicycles.

Those fellows did not own the featherlight multigeared miracles we took for granted, Bob said. They rode brakeless machines that would not coast, earning every foot of forward motion. Those men rode uphill and down in the same gear ratio. Our own riding was so easy that, by comparison, it hardly qualified as training at all.

Bob would get excited describing one of those guys' silky pedaling styles, someone's fearsome sprint or uncanny climbing ability. Certain stories got told more than once, as you'd imagine. They became the stuff of legend.

Bob got most worked up talking about an eastern rider of incalculable class named John Allis. Since Allis never traveled west, he remained shrouded in mystery to us California bikies. He served as a permanent example of New England perseverance and toughness.

Probably we needed examples of toughness. One Sunday morning, one of the juniors, a kid thin as only a 16-year-old can be, gave up and put his bike in his dad's car after a crummy start in a race. He'd been dropped in the first quarter-mile of a fast criterium.

Now, no one went to Bob and told him the kid, Tony, had abandoned. Somehow, without ever appearing at the races, Bob always knew what had happened. He never criticized riders face to face, but he had a way of getting ideas across without a confrontation.

Tony and I and several others were leaning on the workbench in the back at Bob's; Bob was talking about John Allis. Allis, legend had it, was so ruggedly individual that he did *everything* his own way.

He wore several layers of clothing on training rides, summer and winter, purposely overheating himself to prepare for sizzling July and August races.

He scorned "athletic" eating fads. Bob told us Allis once won a bigtime eastern race after dining on several raw hamburgers.

Allis's training consisted of a year-round commute in intemperate Boston and long, hard rides at killing speeds in the New England countryside. Bob said that, though Allis rode a modern derailleur bicycle, he seldom changed gear. Allis preferred to flatten hills with his power; he liked to go faster by pedaling faster.

Mind you, none of us guys would have recognized John Allis if he rode by in the street. Still, he had our respect. If any one in 10 of the stories told about him was true, he was one tough dude.

We'd thought that Bob had told us all the Allis stories he knew, but as we stood there around Bob's bench, he began one we'd never heard. It seems Allis had flatted immediately after the start of some horribly hard road race in the Green Mountains, which Bob said went up and down Vermont.

It took Allis forever to get a replacement wheel. He took off alone, passing rider after rider, catching the pack just before the finish. He rode almost unimpeded through the bunch, sprinted with the leaders, and ended up second by three lengths.

Spectators and riders alike considered him the moral victor, Bob said.

As he finished the story, Bob looked at us all in the room, meeting the eyes of each of us, searching our faces for signs that something of Allis's classy display of grit had sunk in.

I thought at the time that Tony's face looked unusually thoughtful, but I couldn't be sure. I made a mental note to watch him, in case he showed new Allis-style resolve. Sure enough, he missed the break in the Pleasantville road race later that month. He chased like a crazy man but never caught.

Years later, I met John Allis himself in Boston. I told him, as you would've, that I'd witnessed a young rider's transformation from quitter to tiger after Bob told him the story of Allis's momentous chase.

"That's great," Allis said. "You know, when I heard that story, it was about Gino Bartali."

OWEN

WE RODE down that stretch of road where the shoulder is wide, out by the power station. He started talking about Owen. Owen had helped him when he first started cycling, he said.

"I used to ride with my arms too straight, like a lot of guys do," he said. "Owen would ride next to me, whack me in the crook of the arm with his hand, tell me to bend my elbows. He must have done that 50 times.

"I didn't learn any of that stuff easily. I was not a natural bike rider," he said. "Oh, I had an okay bike, and I could pedal all right, but I hadn't a clue how to ride, really.

"I hated to ride a wheel, close behind another person; couldn't see what was ahead. Guy in front might like to ride through craters or run into houses. How could I know?

"Owen said, 'Sit here behind me,' so I did. He saw me using the wrong gear over and over. He had me buy a freewheel cluster just like his. I'd use the same cog he did. Now and then I'd get lazy. He'd ask, 'Why are you in the big chainring?' Took a while, but I figured it out.

"All the while," he said, "Owen was indoctrinating me about bike racing, telling me about rollers and sprinters and climbers. He told me about cycling history and the famous races. He described the cobblestones and mud and the hot stuff the Europeans would rub on their legs so they could race in shorts in freezing weather.

"He told me about a guy who welded his broken fork in the middle of the Tour de France. He told me about a guy who always finished second and another guy who raced so cool and economically that he never dropped anybody but who couldn't be dropped. He told me there were places in the world where a bike rider could be famous.

"He told me how wool clothing keeps you warm even when it's wet with sweat or rain; sure enough, it did. He told me that if I kept my legs warm in cold weather and turned low gears, I wouldn't have knee trouble. So I did, and I haven't."

As we turned north toward the reservoir, he said that Owen kept him away from group rides at first.

"When we finally did start going out with the club," he said, "not only did he continue hassling me about my old bad habits, he began to get on me about pack mistakes. I was new to the sport; when I was feeling my oats I'd go to the front and pull until I was toasted.

"Two or three times like that, and I'd be off the back. Owen would try to say something to me before I got sawed off. Or he'd come back and tow me up, asking me, 'Why'd you do that?' or making some crack about Mr. Horsepower. He must have told me to take short pulls as many times as he told me to bend my elbows.

"When I started riding training races, he'd watch me from his own place in the pack. It used to amaze me. One time he rode up next to me and yelled, 'Up a tooth!' He knew the pace was about to pick up and I'd be in too low a gear to respond. Sometimes he'd point out a good wheel to follow.

"After those events, we'd ride home together and discuss the racing. It frustrated him that it took me so long to learn to read the pack. He'd ask me, 'Didn't you know the bunch would jump?' After a while, a pretty long while, I did.

"After a season or two, in fact, it got to where Owen and I would ride the same races. If the course was really hilly, I could get away and maybe beat him once in a while. Still, he helped me and took pleasure in my success.

"He had a good job that took a lot of his time, so he couldn't train as much as I did. He could always outroll me and certainly outsprint me, even on hardly any miles. My sprint is undetectable by modern scientific instruments.

"I wonder what people do who live where Owen doesn't live. You know what I mean? I wonder how long it takes them to figure all this stuff out. I guess it's easier today; there are lots of books around. But no book is gonna remind you you're in the wrong gear, or point out a strong rider to follow in a bunch sprint.

"Some of these guys who live around here, their hero is the guy who won the criterium over at Pleasantville last week. They don't follow the sport in Europe. It's like they think bike racing got invented just before they bought their bikes. No way Owen would have let me act like that.

"I help guys when I can, but when I think of all the effort he put into helping me, I feel I can never pay it back. A big part of the reason this sport's been so good to me is the time he spent with me when I was green.

"I think I'll call him this afternoon just to say hi," he said. "Oh, incidentally; bend your elbows."

REMEMBER
HOW SLOW?

WE'D LOADED the bikes on the roof, bags in the trunk. We backed the car out of Keith's driveway and set off for the races.

Now, me, I like to listen to the radio while I drive to the races. I get into a meditative state, you might say, listening to familiar songs on the radio. Calms me, the music does. My mind expands, kaleidoscopes; I think of a thousand things. My emotions surface and flash. This stuff only happens to me on the way to races, when I'm alone.

This time, obviously, I'm not alone. Keith is a super guy and a stronger rider than I am, but Keith isn't up for the quiet ride to the road race. Keith likes to talk. I know a little conversation never hurt anyone, but something about Keith's style of chat makes me ill at ease. Like, say, a growing lump on a favorite old silk sew-up would.

"Oh, man," Keith might say, "racing this year is really different than last year."

Keith's been racing every weekend so far this season, while I've been solving problems, like how to pay rent and feed myself.

"Last year I thought the racing was really fast," Keith would say. "You remember, how we'd talk about how fast it was. Well, this year

*'Something about Keith's style of chat makes me ill at ease. Like, say, a growing lump
on a favorite old silk sew-up would.'*

it's *so* much harder. At that criterium last week at Pleasantville, I had to use the big ring all the way up to that turn near the top, where it gets real steep. Last year I could stay in the little ring."

"Really," I say.

"Really," Keith says. "Why, last year the three or four fastest of us would ride off the front and have the race to ourselves. This season there's so *many* fast guys we have to go hard lap after lap, saw 'em off one by one. It's brutal."

"Uh huh," I say.

"And tactics. Last year no one used team tactics in our races. Every man rode for himself. Those days are over. Without help, without guys to block if you get away, without someone to lead you out, you haven't got a chance of a place."

"Is that right?" is my charming reply.

"Oh, no, it's not as simple as it was," Keith goes on. "Not only are guys helping their teammates, they're less honest about how tired they are, or if they can take a pull. A guy could be hanging on like grim death in a break, can't come through and can't speak from being out of breath. Then, miraculously, he can ride the last 200 meters at 35 mph."

"*No,*" I say.

"Yes. And you used to be able to get along with just one skill, the way you do with climbing; not that you can't do *any*thing else. Well, you can't win with just one skill any more. You can't get enough distance on the climbs—you'll get caught. Lots of these guys can really descend and roll. They'll catch you and hammer so hard a pure climber can't hang on. Hey, it's awesome."

"You got any aspirin in the glove box?" I ask.

"No, no aspirin. You got the sun in your eyes? Here, wear my sunglasses," Keith says. "I was thinking about Dupont. Boy, could he roll. Like a train. I remember him spitting one guy after another off his wheel on that long grade last year at districts. He's still rolling just as well, but he gets dropped on the climbs. I mean it; times have changed. A guy's got to have it all to do any good."

"Wow," I say. "Amazing how fast it's changed."

"It is. It is," Keith agrees. "This course we're riding today, we rode it

21

this spring in a practice race. Last year the hills broke everything up; if you got a little gap on a climb you could stay away. No way this year. This year we climbed in the 17 and no one hung around at the top; it was big chainring and hammer-down on the descents. The fitness level has gone up amazingly."

"I see that..."

"What really knocks me out," Keith says, "is the quality of our training rides. If you could make time to get out on more of 'em, you'd see, right away. Just going on those for a few weeks made me racing fit before I knew it."

"Always takes me lots of miles," I say quietly.

"Miles used to do it," Keith suggests. "But miles without quality won't cut it any more. I'm telling you, just being able to ride 23 or 24 mph isn't enough. The pace... the pace."

"I think I have a slow leak in my rear tire," I say.

"I brought a spare wheel with a new cotton; use it," Keith says.

"Probably got the wrong cluster," I suggest.

"I've got a puller in my kit," Keith says. "You can use your own cluster."

"I think my freewheel's Italian thread; probably won't fit."

"So's my hub," Keith says. "You're in luck."

"Right," I say. "Right."

IN THEIR SHOES

ONE YEAR, back when, our little club attracted two sponsors in addition to Bob's shop. A local restaurant, Pucci's, donated money for entry fees and gas money to get us to races. A cycling-shoe importer supplied top-grade cleated shoes to every license holder in the club.

Bob ordered us jerseys with the sponsors' logos on them. I remember feeling sort of bigtime, professional, in my jersey. Getting help from inside *and* outside the bicycle industry made me feel less invisible, less a part of an underground subsport. I squared my skinny shoulders with pride.

The people at Pucci's didn't even suggest we eat there often. The owner, an Italian gentleman from the old country, had raced as a young man; he loved being able to associate himself with the sport.

The shoe company took an order for so many shoes in so many sizes. Then they had to take some back and exchange sizes. No one at the shoe outfit complained; they were happy to give something back to the sport. I believe they liked doing Bob's little club a favor.

All we had to do was wear our jerseys and ride our bikes. That's what we'd have done anyway, except that without Bob and the two new sponsors we'd have had to pay for every darn thing ourselves. I know I liked filling out race entries with all those names: the club, Bob's shop, and the sponsors. Made me and my racing seem important.

As the season went on, it seemed to me some of the guys forgot how grateful they'd been for the help. I heard one guy recommend somebody else's restaurant to a friend visiting with his family. To my mind the other place had no more to offer than Pucci's. I didn't say anything, but I got curious: why wouldn't my clubmate support the people who supported him?

I saw guys racing in old jerseys without our new sponsors' logos. I wondered if they just forgot to bring the new ones. I remember when the jersey shipment ran late, Bob's phone rang off the hook with calls from guys impatient for their new team clothing. Then when they had it they couldn't be bothered to wear it to the races.

Once I watched a guy bring a friend to Bob's to get sized for racing shoes. They left without buying. Later I heard him say he'd told his buddy about a sale at another bike shop. After checking at Bob's, the friend could call the other store and make sure the shoe was in stock in his size.

I saw guys wearing their free shoes and free jerseys, getting Bob to work on their bikes for free, sending people to other stores or recommending other sources or brands of merchandise. You figure it.

Bob must have been aware of this stuff going on, but if it upset him he never let on. I remember the night before our June club meeting, he asked the club president, Cecil, to meet him at Pucci's for dinner. I saw Bob's truck in Pucci's lot late that evening, so the two of them must've had a long talk.

At the club meeting, Cecil waited for a quiet moment and asked us just why we thought our sponsors, Bob and Pucci and the shoe people, had offered us help. "Why would they do that?" he asked. No one had a ready answer.

Cecil asked us if we thought our sponsors would become famous because of us wearing their names on our jerseys. He asked us if we thought they had used that advertising money or work time the most effective way. Couldn't they have used the hours better or spent the money on radio time or in the paper or on a bigger Yellow Pages ad?

He asked us what we thought our sponsors wanted from us. He asked Roger, one of the best riders in the club, why he'd taken a magic marker and blacked over the labels on his shoes, the shoes he'd been so happy to take for free. Roger stammered a little, embarrassed. No answer.

Cecil suggested that maybe the sponsors expected a little loyalty. You didn't have to eat at Pucci's night after night, but you could show a preference if someone asked. Wouldn't hurt to steer a little business their way, huh?

Bob, Cecil said, had been on our side since the beginning. Without Bob, he said, there probably wouldn't be a club. There certainly wouldn't be any new wheels built the night before the districts. Or sew-ups you could pay for on payday after you flatted your last training tire. Or Bob's wisdom or tools or thoughtfulness or sympathy when you needed them.

"What do you think these people expect?" Cecil asked again. "What if you yell an insult at a guy in a car, and he turns out to be Pucci's brother-in-law? What if he's married to the sister of the guy who paid your way to the track races last week? What'll you do for gas money next year? How'll you look at Pucci?

"What if you hate Pucci's food, and the shoes fit terrible, and you think Bob builds crummy wheels? What then? What do you think those people would have you do? You could talk to them. Or maybe you could start rumors about how folks get poisoned at the restaurant, crippled by the shoes, or maybe crash on account of Bob's wheels.... Telling stories like those doesn't sound right, though, does it, but that's just what some of you do.

"Ask yourself," Cecil said, "why Bob helps us so much and never wants a thing. Ask yourself why we all got shoes from some guy who's never met us and who will probably never sell a single extra pair because of us. And why a guy trying to get by running a restaurant would give us money to travel to bike races he'll never see.

"Before you put on your jersey, getting suited up for your next ride," Cecil said, "stop a minute. Think about it. Ask yourself why people do things like that. Imagine you are them. Try it. Do you get the idea?

"Great," Cecil said. "Now go for your ride."

THUD

"THERE WERE witnesses," Mark McCalla said, "who saw the guy swerving down the road. One woman said her daughter was crying in the back seat of her car, certain the man would hit them and kill them, mother and child.

"This guy had two prior drunk-driving convictions. Both times he got his license back," McCalla said. "Now, he'll probably get off again without hardly any jail time, and Billy's dead."

McCalla said Billy had been 17, just about to graduate from high school and a genius, especially in math.

"He was a really nice kid, getting to be a good bike racer. He was on his way home from this Thursday-evening training race we have, when the guy hit him. Killed him instantly," McCalla told me.

"I skipped the race myself. Decided to stay home and ride the wind trainer. It was kind of a crummy night, windy and raining, but Billy rode to the race and rode home. I was in the process of buying a new car, and I stayed out late wrangling with the guy I was buying it from. I didn't hear anything until the next morning.

"A lawyer I know who happened to know the guy's lawyer called me, asked me if I'd heard about Billy. I thought he'd crashed or something. The lawyer said Billy'd been in an accident. I asked if he'd been hurt or anything. The lawyer said he understood Billy was dead.

"It took me quite a while to get all the details," McCalla said. "It seems the driver heard a thud that night, in the rain, you know. He got scared the next morning when he thought about it—scared he might have hurt somebody.

"So he called his bartender. The bartender knew a lawyer. Put this guy in touch with the lawyer. Lawyer told the guy, 'Don't say anything.' Guy turns himself in to the lawyer; they go down to the police station. Set the process of justice in motion.

"They plea-bargain the case, is what they call it," McCalla told me. "They do a dance for a while, the attorneys, then the guy pleads guilty to a charge of operating a motor vehicle in a fashion most untidy, or interfering with the serenity of the neighborhood. The judge feints toward the guy's wrist with an imaginary ruler and he walks. Later that day, he drives.

"I feel terrible," McCalla said. "What can I do? You can tell people to be careful, not to crash. You can tell people to glue their tires on, about what happens when you roll one off the rim. But what can you say about someone like this? It's got me looking back over my shoulder.... I hate to think there's another drunk out there like this one, gonna hit somebody and not even know he did it.

"We started a training series for juniors, named it after Billy," McCalla said. "He hadn't been riding a long time, but he'd made a lot of friends around here."

McCalla said that even if only a bunch of bikies read this, there might be one or two who drink and drive once in a while, or know someone who does.

He said, "This thing has put me off my bike. I've hardly ridden for quite some time now."

I told McCalla I thought it was great that Billy had had a friend like him. McCalla said he kept trying to remember the good times he and Billy'd had. He said that was all he could do.

WENDY

"WHEN I first started coming out with you guys," Wendy said, "I was not having a good time. I liked the idea, you know, of training with the men, learning how to ride a wheel and get along in a paceline. The reality of the rides, though, was not good.

"I always got dropped," she said. "I got dropped on the flats when the hammer fell. I got dropped on long gentle upgrades when guys would decide to use the big chainring.

"But mostly, I got dropped on the climbs. I can't tell you how many times I got left alone on some hill, watching half a dozen of you guys pedal effortlessly away.

"I felt slow and I felt fat," Wendy said. "Each time, I'd think: this is a futile effort. I'm never going to be good enough. You guys would always ride away, chatting amiably among yourselves while I struggled to the top of the hill.

"I wasn't fat, really," she said. "In fact, I didn't weigh any more than I do now. I just couldn't make the bike go fast enough. If you remember, during that time I was seeing David a lot. He never exactly asked me to train with the guys, but I liked the idea of sharing an athletic activity, and I liked being with him.

"So I borrowed Susan's bike, and I got sawed off a mile and a half into the ride.

"I guess I didn't truly understand the level of suffering. I'd seen David come home sweaty and exhausted; I knew we weren't headed for the country with picnic baskets. Still, I underestimated the agony.

"Why I kept coming back, I don't know," Wendy said. "I guess I thought that if a man could do it, a woman could do it too. I couldn't see anything about a bicycle that favored one sex over the other.

"By the time David quit riding, I'd bought my own bike. I was pretty committed to finishing those rides in the group. I could've quit easily myself, but there was No Way. I was still getting dropped, and getting angry and frustrated, but I was not giving up.

"It would be neat to say that I persevered and got fitter and fitter, and finally I hung in. It didn't happen that way. Bob helped me a lot during that time. He'd always been nice to me when I came in the shop, but he never took a personal interest until David quit turning up for the rides.

"One day at the shop he asked me how my riding was going. I felt particularly defeated at the time, so I unloaded all my helplessness and resentment on him. Bob listened sympathetically but didn't say much.

"If I'd looked to him for a quick magic cure, I'd have been disappointed. He said he'd try to keep an eye on me when he could.

"Two days later," Wendy said, "Bob showed up for the ride. On the flat, the fast part out there by the dam, I started to drift off the back, like usual. I was three bikelengths back when Bob appeared next to me pointing at his back wheel.

"I had just enough left to jump into his draft. It took three tries, but eventually he dragged me back up to the group. I was cooked, but I was jubilant.

"I began to understand the necessity of the draft, the need to be on a wheel, in the shelter of the pack. That understanding helped me; I started to hang in better on the flats. Bob would come out once or twice a week and coach me.

"He'd say, 'Close that gap,' or, 'Why are you in such a big gear?' He taught me to save energy, to relax when I could so I'd have something in reserve for the crunches.

"The hills," Wendy said, "the hills were another matter. I'd got to where I could make it to the bottoms of the climbs with the guys, but then.... Anyway, one day Bob dropped back to me, where I usually was, about 20 uphill yards behind the pack. 'Jump the distance and sit in,' he said. 'The group is only going a little faster than you are.' I glared at him; obviously he didn't understand that I was maxed out. 'Come on,' he said.

"I jumped as hard as I could and gained back about half the distance. I could scarcely breathe. Bob reached over and put his hand on the back of my saddle and pushed me to the pack.

"I fixated on a wheel and hung on as fiercely as I could. When I'd begin to lose the wheel, Bob would heave me back up. The effort was unbelievable, but so was the thrill of reaching the top of the hill with the guys. And starting down the other side without having to chase.

"Now, obviously, it didn't suddenly get easy for me to hang in on the hills. But, from then on I knew, I *knew*, that I could do it. It's not like I don't hardly get a workout today, but I have a little left now, even when you guys get kinda competitive, like today.

"And once in a while, I get to give a little bit back. Last week, you remember the guy in the red jersey, wearing a brand new yellow hat? Well, he started to drift off the back on Pinehurst Hill, up where it gets steep.

"Well, I couldn't get him to bridge by talking to him. I grabbed his saddle and pushed him to the top. It felt good to be able to do that," Wendy said.

"When the guy looked back at me to say thanks, I smiled at him like Bob would've. After the ride, he came over and thanked me again. 'That's okay,' I told him. 'I've been off the back myself.' "

MILES

"HELLO...."

"Hi, Frank, it's Jim. How you doin'?"

"Good, Jim. How 'bout you? You over that flu yet?"

"Mostly over it, but it sure is hanging on a long time. I think maybe I'm a little overtrained."

"No kidding? Are you getting in lots of miles?"

"Not *that* many, really, but they're all quality miles. No pain, no gain, right? I'm not sleeping all that well. I have this recurring nightmare: I'm crossing the finish line alone, arms above my head, winning Milan–San Remo after a 100-kilometer solo break. Then I wake up to realize I'm just the first guy to the lunch stop in the Pottsville Pedal Pushers Metric Century."

"Oh, that's a bad one."

"Really. And I think maybe I'm getting a little too thin. I got on a bus down on Grant Street yesterday, and this little girl saw me and screamed. Oh, and my dog, Fausto—my basset? I came home from a ride Tuesday, and Fausto didn't recognize me, took a nip out of my leg, tore my good tights. Upset me."

"Geez, that's too bad. Poor Fausto."

"Well, my jersey might have had something to do with it. I got this old Look jersey, might have belonged to Bernard Hinault. I resist washing it; might have a little of the old magic still in it. Who knows?"

"How'd you get so overtrained?"

"I thought this year I'd really see if I could do it. I wouldn't hold back or compromise. I decided this was the season I would make my mark, get out of Cat IV and possibly get a Cat III placing or two. So far, no good. I think maybe my early-season training was ill advised...."

"Hey, I remember. Running those stadium steps in full field pack, with the bike on your shoulder...."

"Oh, yeah, back in December. That worked out okay, but in January I ran the stairs in Montgomery Towers downtown in a wetsuit and ankle weights. That was hard. End of January I got shin splints, couldn't run any more, started training seriously on the bike.

"I'd ride short in the mornings, maybe do a few sprints, sometimes a 15-kilometer time trial. I'd come home and eat a light meal, maybe pump a little iron. Then I'd go down to the Y and swim a lap or two. In the afternoons I'd get on the bike and do a real workout."

"Jim, that sounds like an awful lot."

"It wasn't so bad, really. It would have been lots easier if I'd been eating normally. I was trying to take off a few pounds, give myself a break on those hills. I got pretty hungry, and a little grouchy—I admit it. It was during that period that I bit Fausto. And my mother moved out so suddenly, after living in that house for 17 years. She'd never even mentioned wanting an apartment. She was just gone."

"You must've been getting super fit about then...."

"Well, sorta fit. I was starting to do longer rides, trying to cross at least two state lines every day. I'd ride in wool sweaters and leg warmers on the hot days, and not carry water. Paying my fitness dues, you might say. I wanted the hardest bike race to seem like a rest day."

"Learning how to suffer, eh?"

"No, that wasn't so bad, in fact. In March I started following my brother-in-law on his motorcycle. At first we'd go about 50 miles at, say, 35 mph. I'd try to jump around the motor every mile or so.

"Later, we'd pick up the speed. I'd ride a 63-inch fixed-gear bike with heavy steel wheels and soft tires. When I felt strong, I'd adjust

'I want plenty of miles in my legs when I start training for real.'

the front brake to drag. We'd quit when my brother-in-law got exhausted. Whew, when I think of trying to breathe, sitting behind that worn-out old two-stroke of his...."

"Didn't the racing start in March?"

"Yeah, some of the early-season events. I just didn't go. I'd think about the race and how hard all the guys were training, and I'd just not go. There's a bunch of guys who ride every morning from a shop here in town. I don't even go with them.

"I see 'em out there. They have a good time, talk a little bit, do some jumps. I've thought about training with them, but I don't know if I'm really ready. I think I need a little more speed."

"After all that motorpacing? You must have terrific speed."

"I have *some* speed, I guess. I don't have enough base. I want plenty of miles in my legs when I start training for real. I'm not interested in showing up at a race just to get dropped on the first hill. Some of those guys are really serious."

"You sound pretty serious yourself."

"Well, I am in my way, but I think I'm doing something wrong. I'm sleeping so badly; last night I had this nightmare that was so bad that when I got woken up by a charley horse I was grateful. I've been kinda hard to get along with. Fausto stays out longer and longer these days.

"I've been thinking about cutting down my reps at the gym, maybe do fewer squats until my resting pulse rate settles back down. That wouldn't be so bad; a few days with normal pulse, and I could pick up the miles on the bike.

"Mileage is what I need. If I was sleeping better and riding more miles, I'd be ready. Hey, I want to be ready. Some of those guys are serious."

CHOICES

BILL, WHO told me this story, said it sounds like it's about people, but it isn't. It's about the System, he explained. The System steamrollers right over individuals; the System denies them their options.

A young man came into Bill's bicycle store several years ago to purchase a leather hairnet-style helmet for his girlfriend, a bicycle racer. The boyfriend sometimes shopped at the store, but Bill couldn't remember the woman ever being there.

For the previous year or so, Bill had stopped selling hairnets, thinking the then-new hard-shell helmets just had to work better. Even so, customers demanded hairnets. Bill stocked some but decided that anyone who bought one at his store would do it over his strongest objections.

He himself wore a "geeky-looking" hard-shell and practiced his principles across his sales counter, promoting helmets and trying to discourage hairnet buyers.

Bill asked the young man to consider a better helmet, one that could really protect his girlfriend if she crashed. The customer explained that his friend intended just to comply with U.S. Cycling Federation regulations, and the federation deemed the hairnet adequate. So that's what he bought. Bill never saw the helmet again.

Later that year, the woman crashed in a USCF-sanctioned event. Her head sustained severe damage. Bill said she is not expected ever to recover completely, ever to be just like she'd been before. He said he understands she incurred around $3 million in medical costs.

Two years after the crash, the woman's insurance company notified Bill that he was being sued, along with the cycling federation, for the $3 million.

Also named in the suit were 50 John Does, representing anyone the insurance company's lawyers felt they could implicate, from whom they could recover part of the money. Some of those John Does could be other racers, or the people who laid out the race course, or corner workers...anybody.

Since the year the helmet was sold, Bill had changed insurance companies. His old company, the one that had insured him at the time of the sale, hired him a lawyer. Bill was further advised to hire another lawyer to represent his personal interests, to protect him from exposure to a possibly huge later claim of liability from his old insurance company.

That made two lawyers; one Bill paid for, and one his insurance policy paid for.

Bill felt that as the reluctant seller, years earlier, of the helmet, he had minimal responsibility for the damage.

"Let's go in," he told his attorneys, "and lay the cards on the table. I had nothing to do with the woman's head injuries. I told them not to buy that helmet. Even if I hadn't, anyone could *see* that it was just a piece of foam rubber, that it couldn't work."

Now, Bill says, he recognizes how naive he was.

He sat through two long, uncomfortable grilling sessions called depositions. Lawyers from the woman's insurance company asked him personal questions, some repeated again and again, trying to determine if he was worth going after for part of the money. Bill found those sessions truly distasteful. In fact, he had just walked away from a divorce empty-handed in order to avoid the same sort of third degree.

Bill did not own a home at the time and had no assets worth the effort of attaching. At that point, however, his insurance company decided to settle, for an amount Bill estimates as the typical maximum liability they provided bike shops then, $300,000.

Bill's insurance company then tried to recover *its* money, first from the boyfriend, then from the distributor who'd sold the helmet to Bill, and finally from the manufacturer. Bill looked through his invoices and could not find one for the helmet. The insurance company subpoenaed his paperwork and uncovered an invoice listing the sale of such an item, not necessarily the woman's one.

The supplier, an old-time, small, bicycle-clothing distributor, was the last person Bill would have wished trouble on.

"He probably hates to hear my name," Bill said. "I'm sure they hassled him. He probably made a buck and a half on that helmet."

The helmet's South American manufacturer escaped entanglement. The company failed to respond to letters or calls. Bill said he thinks the lawyers considered it uneconomical to try to collect from a foreign company.

Bill told me he feels sorry for the woman now, but at one time he was angry. He blamed her for all the trouble.

"She's the one who decided to wear that hairnet. It was totally and clearly not my fault. There's no way it could be. What if you bought a sweatshirt at Penney's and went on an expedition to Mt. Everest, got frostbite, and lost your arms? Would you come home and sue Penney's, claiming the sweatshirt was inadequate because it didn't keep you warm?

"That experience turned me around. I'm an old Boy Scout; I used to believe in right and wrong. A lawyer told me to stop being such a wimp—this is the way things work. It's not got to do with right and wrong. It's got to do with people making a lot of money and with things that are a lot bigger than you and me.

"It's true someone had to pay her medical bills. We're in a risky sport; we take chances. Obviously, she took more of a chance than was sensible. At least if she'd have crashed in a hard-shell helmet and been hurt, she'd have taken all the care she could.

"That experience made me aware of the risks we take. Now I have a personal insurance policy that covers me in case of catastrophic injury. I'm covered for a lot of money. I feel I take responsibility for myself, having that policy.

"People think when they take chances they're making simple individual choices, placing only themselves at risk. The fact is they're placing their families, their bike shop, their friends, everybody, at risk. They no longer control the risk if their medical bills surpass their financial responsibility.

"That woman never said it was my fault she got hurt. I'm sure she doesn't think it *was* my fault. She was forced to sue me to recover her medical costs. She probably had as much grief or more than I did over it. Every rider should ask him or herself, 'Do I want to end up in that situation? Do I want to end up hurt in some hospital, suing people I know and probably like, because I was too cool to wear a helmet?' "

FLIP

FLIP WAS legendary here. He grew up in our area, then left to ride on national teams and race in places so remote and romantic they seemed almost fantasy. He quit racing years ago, but he kept riding his bike. When he needed a tire or a cable he'd come to Bob's shop.

Flip had raced on teams of big-name riders, names familiar to bikies all over the country. He'd done great things. He'd been leading overall in a stage race in France when his frame broke, far from support, forcing him to abandon.

He had a "King of the Mountains" jersey he'd won in another French stage race. He had stories we could never get enough of.

If you were a bike racer, you'd want Flip for a teammate. He would willingly give you his spare tire or his bicycle. He could ride the wrong size bike or one that had crummy brakes or wouldn't shift. He rode for the team, as selflessly as a saint. He had a perfectly even temperament. Soft-spoken as he was, when he arrived at Bob's, he drew a crowd.

I remember six or seven of us standing in a circle asking Flip provocative questions, hoping to get him telling stories. We talked about training for a while, then about racing, then about specific races. Flip told two of my favorite stories that afternoon; I'll try to retell them as faithfully as I can.

Flip recalled he'd raced in southern California, in a road race on a six-mile circuit. The field had been large and sluggish. Flip jumped away on a hill, taking another guy with him. Flip's teammates went to the front of the pack and shut it down; the two had a gap right away.

Flip knew nothing about his breakaway partner. Even though they had several laps of the circuit to ride, the partner refused to help. He wouldn't pull through. Each time Flip moved over to let him take a turn, the man would quit pedaling.

As you can imagine, Flip quickly became frustrated and suggested to the guy that perhaps two working partners might have a better chance of staying away than one worker would.

The wheel-sucker saw, evidently, that Flip's teammates had slowed the field so that one man's efforts might just be enough. He might just sit in and finish fresh, maybe fresh enough to come around Flip for the win.

He decided, evidently, to gamble on Flip's rolling ability; he sat in and contributed nothing at all. The course was pretty flat, so Flip couldn't ride away from the guy on a hill. Nor could he try to attack on flat road. The partner was enjoying a free ride, resting. Flip knew that he could tire himself so badly trying to drop the man that he might be caught by the pack.

As I listened to Flip telling the story, I imagined myself in that same predicament. I wondered what I'd do. Flip stopped his story to say hi to someone who'd come into Bob's. As soon as his eyes got distant and thoughtful again, one of us asked him what he'd done.

"I stopped," he said. "We were riding up the steepest hill on the course. I waited until about two thirds of the way up, and I stopped on the hill, kind of like a match sprinter would, and I looked back at the guy.

"It surprised him so much," Flip said, "he muffed his track stand. He almost fell over before he could reach down, loosen a toestrap, and put a foot down.

"As soon as I saw his foot hit the ground, I jumped as hard as I could. I never looked back. I guess the guy must've felt terrible about getting dropped. He got reeled in by the pack and did nothing in the field sprint."

Now, Flip left out the part about how he finished alone, a minute and a half up on a hard-chasing pack. He told another story, though, about a well-known eastern road sprinter we'll call Bill. Bill entered a multilap road race in an area of the country where he wasn't recognized.

The pack watched a four-man break ride up the road. The break got out of sight and, apparently, out of mind. No one wanted to chase.

Bill attacked out of a corner and got a gap of a few bikelengths. He put his head down and made good his escape, hammering for all he was worth. Soon he could see the break. He composed himself as he made contact. He told the group he was a *lapped rider*. He would sit in, if they didn't mind, and help out the break.

What Bill did to help, mostly, was sit at the back. Probably he took a couple of pulls, just to justify his presence in the break. And, just as you'd expect, he was so well rested by the last lap, when he jumped at 300 meters, no one had a prayer of grabbing his wheel.

Flip imitated the guy, crossing the line, grinning, hands in the air. Then Flip's face went neutral; we could make up our own minds about the guy and his tactics. I think the story stunned us all.

I tried to imagine a bike-racing world where a guy could do stunts like that one and expect people to forget and not tell the story. I couldn't imagine one.

I thought about the things some people will do to win. I thought about how badly some folks need to beat other folks, at any cost. After a while, thinking about it got old. I rolled out of Bob's into the afternoon sun.

MYBIKE: THE TEST

EACH SPARKLING new bicycle placed in this writer's brutal but mechanically sensitive hands for road testing generates new excitement and raises new questions. The Mybike Myway, this month's feature bike, in particular qualifies as a genuine traditional classic, at a time when many sport-cycling enthusiasts consider tradition (per se) roughly as desirable as a softening rear tire.

Cicli Mybike, manufacturers of the Mybike Myway, fabricate what might amount to thousands of units yearly, one by one, in the old, hands-on Italian fashion.

Fabricate may be a crude term to describe the loving care lavished by the Mybike family on these polished steel gems. Indeed, as each chrome and gleaming enamel example is wrapped for shipment, the Mybike clan gathers for a brief farewell. Many times, often, tears are shed.

Mybike workers include Ing Mybike, his three sons, and the youngest son's close friend, Marco. The five carefully select and cut tubing, lovingly braze and file and prepare and paint the modest factory's output. Mybike production has been estimated at either 350 bikes per year or 350 bikes per day, depending on who you ask. An exact figure is difficult to determine and certainly meaningless. Craftsmanship is as craftsmanship does, and Mybike does it good.

Mybike handling qualities include on-a-rail tracking, almost as if the headset were too tight, and a high-strung, joyous agility. Frame geometry and construction integrity combine with the rider's caffeine consumption level to produce serendipitously disparate handling characteristics. The bicycle tracks perfectly hands-off only if loaned to other, cleverer riders. In this test rider's one no-hands experience, it veered suddenly into the prickerbushes alongside the road. That experience momentarily alarmed and superficially wounded this tester but provided evident mirth to his lowlife training partners for days afterward. Wankers.

Mybike's frame angles precisely interpret the Italian philosophy of stability and reassurance. Each time one gazes at the bike, each time one mounts it on his roofrack, each time one rides it, under any (*any!*) imaginable circumstance, without fail the Mybike frame angles vary not a degree. Not one.

That sort of dependability, in what may be an uncertain age, instills a sense of confidence in a Mybike owner. He can sense that if his unique Italian masterpiece steered flawlessly yesterday it will steer flawlessly again today. What price that sort of confidence? With it, one can play tennis, water-ski, descend like a crazy person on rain-slick blacktop, wear a leisure suit—anything.

Each Mybike frameset is carefully constructed of the same tubing designated by every other Italian thoroughbred exotic builder you can name. Each emerges from the tiny Mybike manufacturing complex (smaller than Fiat, larger than Alfa Romeo) a light, compact, responsive unit. Each ignites blazes of expectation in the newly impoverished but superheated owner.

Unfortunately, each light, compact frameset requires for use installation of wheels, brakes, bars, stem, changers—you know. So it ends up about the same size and weight as all those other bikes after all. Still, a nice try.

The European equipment complementing our Mybike test machine seemed remarkably well chosen in appearance and action. This tester felt the component choices matched his own preferences with almost telepathic faithfulness. Many cyclists, however, some with up to three full seasons of biking workouts, seemed surprised to see the European parts on a current machine. One suggested it might be a beautifully restored '50s-vintage mount. Such charming comments from fellow enthusiasts add imperceptibly to an owner's pride of possession.

The test bike's gearing shrugged off every challenge local terrain could serve up except for the ill-timed off-road excursion mentioned above. A lower bottom gear might have enabled our tester to have ridden the bike cyclocross-fashion out of the gully, back up to the road. Perhaps a show of a certain brave style might have saved a few (scratched) square centimeters of face. Alas.

The Mybike handlebar/stem combination fit this pitiless bike-breaker perfectly. The bars, wrapped in this cyclojournalist's favorite tape, felt directly connected to the steering, as if alloy forging linked the two. Stem length and brake lever placement, fussy individual preferences, couldn't have been improved. For instance, the right-hand lever controlled the front brake. Bravo. Entirely to taste, Mybike builders.

Gear changing on the Mybike test model proved instantly familiar: our rider felt at home at once. The shift levers fell, as some lesser testers might suggest, readily to hand. Requisite overshifting on changes up the cluster never intruded during the several grueling training marathons to which this Kong-thighed tubing-twister subjected the bike.

The all-important wheels on our test Mybike featured the highly regarded, heat-treated, hard-anodized, surface-toughened, quick-release-handle-attachment nut lockwashers. It is just this sort of expensive attention to detail that is easily missed by the untrained, nonbicycle-tester eye. Such touches typify the sometimes subtle value that aficionados prize in Italian industrial masterworks of pedigree.

The Mybike wheels, tubular rims spoked to polished alloy precision-bearing hubs, roll smoothly. Perhaps more important, those wheels prevent the bright chrome Mybike dropouts from scraping on the ground. And bottom bracket height, regarded by experts as a fundamental determinant of bicycle handling qualities, depends entirely on the installation of these wheels. If you don't learn a single other thing from this article, remember *that*.

Tubular tires provide the Mybike with a lively ride. The responsive

The Mybike workers carefully select and cut tubing, lovingly braze and file, prepare and paint the modest factory's output.

tubular "feel" (*blush*) cannot be approached by easier-to-deal-with clinchers, even clinchers costing several times as much as the undistinguished sew-ups on our Mybike sample.

This tester found the admittedly pedestrian tubulars to have been mounted solidly on the Mybike rims. As evidence, red rim cement had bubbled onto the coarse, low-budget sidewalls, somewhat marring the overall esthetic aspect of one of Milan's proudest industrial moments. As always, perfection eludes us.

Riding our test Mybike revealed its chameleonlike (is that a cliche?) adaptability. On days when the rider felt strong, eager, and competitive, the bicycle leapt forward at the most tentative pedal pressure.

On other days, when this bicycle-bruising road tester trained with young, impertinent junior racers, the Mybike Italian *objet d'art* responded sluggishly: dead slow. Careful checking of tire pressures and bearing adjustment availed nothing. Curious. No, the brake pads cleared the rims just fine.

Paint and chrome gild the Mybike lily, gorgeously hiding the painstaking handiwork of the builders. The enamel and plating, lavishly, though somewhat temporarily, applied in appalling conditions right in the tiny Mybike Industrial Park, shout *Viva Italia* to the true believer.

The turquoise enamel, designated Bartali Blue, elicited raves from other cyclists. One rider after another hesitated while passing this tester on uphill grinds. Each one spoke glowingly about the classic Mybike beauty. Each admired the glistening paint and chrome and the unusual polished accessories before accelerating effortlessly, infuriatingly away.

Most were baffled and envious at the eerie silence of the gear changes. The chain moved whisper-quiet from the middle cogs up to larger ones on the climb as this bicycle-testing bronze god settled into a rhythmic, mile-eating cadence. Overtaking cyclists stared in awed disbelief. *Why doesn't it click?* they wondered.

THE RIGHT THING

I ADMIT it, I had last-lap jitters. I'm no criterium rider, and it sure was a criterium: six turns per three-quarter-mile lap, flat as a new chainring. Not my style; still, I'd hung in okay—24 laps behind me and one to go.

In the spring, I can finish these races in the pack. No one's raging fit, itching to risk forcing the pace that early in the year. If you take a hard pull and move over, no one'll come through. The good part is everybody finishes; the bad part is the whole pack goes around corners together and sprints together. Crowded corners and bunch sprints mean danger for green, eager bike racers.

Last lap. Here we go. I bumped the lever and got the 14, thinking the final-lap pace would quicken. Everybody behaved in the first corner and the second. I had to get out of the saddle to get the 14 going out of each corner; felt good. I liked the effort, liked moving the bike a little under myself, feeling the power, getting psyched for the sprint.

On the back straight guys jockeyed for position, about what you'd expect. I sat around fifth going into the corner, on the inside, right where I wanted to be. I heard someone yell, "Inside, inside." A rider came up from behind, maybe 5 mph faster than me, right up the curb.

I couldn't believe my eyes. How could he expect to make it around the corner, without any arc, without being able to sweep through? Then I was in the corner, and guys were falling in front of me. I straightened up my bike and rode off the pavement and up a rocky embankment, hanging on for dear life. Ride 'em, bikie.

I ended up stopped on a grassy ledge, staring down at the fallen riders, astonished I hadn't crashed myself.

The war was over for me. By the time I could hear over the sound of my heart, the crowd at the finish line was cheering the winner. People ran over to ask the crashed guys and me if we were all right. I said I was fine. My rear tire was a casualty, though. A brand-new silk, wouldn't you know. The downed racers grumbled, disgusted, in short Anglo-Saxon incantations.

The first guy who fell said the gentleman who'd passed me so suddenly cut him off. He'd gone into the turn on the inside and needed the whole width of the road on the way out. The first guy down took out the second, the two landing in a sad heap together.

They'd gotten similarly scraped up, their elbows and feelings red and angry. They said they planned to protest the fellow's unsafe riding, right away.

I took off my cycling shoes and started the long walk back to the start/finish. As I walked my bike, my shoes tucked under my arm, I sorted out my feelings about what happened. I hadn't expected to finish well (my sprint is nearly nonexistant) but, what the heck, I'd made it *that* far.

When I got close to the crowd of spectators, someone ran out and told me that the fellow who'd caused the crash had, in fact, won the race. Gee. I looked at my destroyed tire, still trying to figure things out.

One of the injured guys stepped up and asked me what I'd seen. I told him about the guy's sudden move up the inside and about my off-road episode. He said the two of them intended to protest formally. Would I sign?

I had to say I hadn't seen the crash happen; I couldn't precisely name the cause. Any evidence I could attest to would be circumstantial. He said the two of them had spoken to Ed, the aggressive guy, and Ed had been proud of his win. He'd said he felt that his hard-charging action was justified.

The injured guy fiddled with his new elbow pad. Clearly disappointed with me, he walked back to the officials' table to continue the protest.

I felt confused and frustrated. I tried to decide what Bob, our shop owner, a guy I truly admire, would do. Bob could get to the bottom of this thing, I thought. The thinking about Bob calmed my mind. I leaned my bike into a hedge and went over to talk to Ed.

"Hey," I said to him. "All right. You won the bike race." He nodded and said he was pleased. I said a couple of guys were protesting; they'd asked me to sign. I told him I hadn't exactly seen what happened, but I thought that his move in the corner was awful bold.

"Really? Did you?" he said. I said I really did. I told him that if we'd been professionals, trying to put food on the table, it might have been less of a surprise. In a vacuum, I said, he could go around the corner any way he wanted, on an empty road, say.

But in a pack of amateur bikies, on the last lap of an early-season criterium.... Why, even if he didn't hit anyone, he'd shock enough guys virtually to guarantee a crash.

"Do you think so?" he asked. I said I did. He said he'd ridden the early laps at the front, then dropped back and sat in. He'd felt rested and eager to get positioned well for the sprint. I said I'd had the same ambition myself.

"Do you think I did the wrong thing?" he asked.

"Well, that's up to you," I said. "What do you think?"

He said he'd found himself at the very back of the pack on the straight before the crash corner. He'd pulled his foot out of his toeclip. Then he had agony getting the shoe back in. By the time he'd done it he'd gotten excited and charged up.

He decided, he said, to come out of the corner in front, so he could control the pack speed for the sprint.

He said he felt he was doing the right thing, at the time. He asked me if I'd fallen. I said no, but you should have seen the other guys. He asked me was I sure I was okay; could he buy me a new tire? I said, hey, one of those things. Thanks, he said.

I watched as he walked over to the judges' table. Later I heard the original race winner had been disqualified; the other placers moved up.

I loaded up and drove home feeling at peace with myself. I couldn't sense any resentment at missing the sprint. I tuned in a country music station that came in real clear and sang along all the way home.

Monday morning I told Bob the same story I just told you, except I left out the part about how I'd tried to figure what he'd have done. No use embarrassing him.

He must have liked the story, though. Bought me this new silk tire.

PELOTONIA

LONG AGO—so long ago in fact that John Howard had only ridden maybe 40 miles in a day, maximum—there existed a magical kingdom called Pelotonia. Pelotonia looked a lot like the place you live, dear reader, except downhillier, tailwindier, curvyroadier—and no one had flatted a tire for years.

Sounds great, huh? It was great, but all was not perfect in Pelotonia. The heir to the throne, or Mustard Mantle, as it was known to the *tifosi*, or peasants, was without a wife. The beloved Dave S. Finely, renowned for his courtly *coup de pedale* and imperial field sprint, had, sadly, been unable to select a lifetime teammate for the royal two-up time trial.

Finely rode every highway and byway in the land, on fixed wheel and free, hoping to meet Regina Right and perhaps develop a little leg speed. Alas, his efforts proved thankless, and he went through lots of chains in wet weather.

Soon he returned to riding what was known as the Criterium Circuit, at which events if he didn't always win, well, he made a living.

Finely, unmarried, could not ascend the vacant throne. In fact, some mornings it was uncomfortable even to ascend the imperial Brooks Processional, which is what fast royalty rode in those beknighted days. Meanwhile, anarchy ruled in Pelotonia.

Anarchy—yes, anarchy—reigned in the little kingdom. Wheels were built five-speed, six-speed, and front brakes hooked up to the right side, to the left side. People rode in double pacelines, single pacelines, and diagonal pacelines. Some wore jerseys with pockets on the *front*.

Craftspersons made frames out of any damn thing. You could buy lawn furniture made from surplus name-brand chrome-moly tubes at trendy imported-housewares stores. People became obsessed with concepts of the merest triviality, like empty calories or rolling resistance. Previously sensible citizens would throw their bikes down after rides, change their shoes, and *run*. Imagine.

It was as if a strange spell hung over the land. Where was Finely to set it right? And where was his regal lead-out?

After a village bike-racing festival in rustic Somerville, Finely fell into a deep sleep during his post-victory massage. In a dream, a solidly built man with a thick northern European accent, remarkably unsoftened by years in the U.S., spoke.

He said: "Not so many miles, Dave S. More quality. Stay closer to home. Take an easy day, a hard day. Maybe see if you can find someone fits this shoe...."

Finely awakened abruptly. Under the massage table he found a beautiful white patent leather cycling shoe, a very small size. He instinctively knew what he had to do—he had to take a leak. After that, and a shower, he said to himself, I'll go investigate my options in size 37½, medium.

He carried the shoe with him always, on training rides and to races. That struck many people as weird, but few spoke up; Finely would, after all, rule Pelotonia one day. He tried the shoe on one dewy-eyed maiden after another. To some he seemed simply an aristocratic nuisance. Others, he grossed *totally* out.

Soon just the sight of ankle socks drove Finely into a frenzy. He would sight a woman rider far up the road, chase in huge gears for miles, only to find (after dinner) that she had a long, narrow foot. And occasionally (gosh), a fallen arch. In the process of his search, Finely lost a measure of dignity and some of his spin.

Summers, Finely and 45 of his *domestiques* (racing friends), practiced bunch sprints for city limit signs. Since there were only four cities in Pelotonia, widely separated by perfect roads, these exercises ran back and forth for the same signs.

The pack would roll down the road, then hammer for about a half mile. Then Finely would give the signal, partly unzipping his skinsuit. Two hundred meters from the line, 45 men would start to soft-pedal. Photos would show Finely winning by trucklengths, time after time. He never tired of this scenario.

One Friday, though, Finely was foiled in his fervor to be first. A tall, willowy, auburn-tressed beauty rode up to the 46 accelerating men, shot straight to the front, and matched Finely pedal stroke for pedal stroke. The unknown woman beat Finely to the line by a carefully practiced bike-throw. Finely waved off the photographers.

"I'm looking," she said, "for the common, cowardly wheel-sucker who stole one of my lucky cycling shoes from the massage tent at the Somerville town fair. Got any ideas, your eventual highness?" she asked angrily, not, however, for one moment forgetting her place.

"As it happens," Finely replied, his heart racing, "I may have that shoe. Is it a white patent Italian custom with a small scrape from a toestrap buckle and a knotted broken lace? I have it here, in a specially designed pocket in the royal racing suit."

Before he knew it, Finely had been hooked off the roadway and deposited (softly) in a muddy ditch. The auburn-haired woman jumped down into the ditch, took the shoe, remounted, and sped off. She easily outdistanced her pursuers, whose big-gear abilities had been eroded by all that soft-pedaling.

As it happened, one of Finely's men had, while racing in far-off track meetings, heard tales of the fleet redhead. Candy Carr-Painter, as she was known, had burned many a strong man off her wheel. She had been bested by no one (well, maybe not *no* one; everyone has an off-day). It was said about Carr-Painter that she could roll, she could climb, and, verily, she could sprint like crazy. The woman had everything.

Finely himself, as soon as he had straightened his handlebars and whacked his saddle back in line, resolved he must have her. "That was

The village of Cannon-dale—where the men are strong and handsome, the women are strong and pretty, and the welds are, well, just strong.

my future wife," he told the boys, "who just put me in the cheap seats."

Right away, Finely sent out roving packs of his henchmen to discover Carr-Painter's favorite training routes. These men were disguised in plain woolen jerseys and off-brand eye protection. They were instructed never to tarry at convenience stores for sweet crushed-ice drinks.

A few sightings had the redhead's rides mapped out. Now all Finely had to do was catch her.

He began training in Earnest, a flat section of southern Pelotonia. He rode in fast pacelines in a very low fixed gear. Soon, his leg speed started to come back. He took pace behind the only motorcycle in Pelotonia, a maniacally ridden turbo-charged Kawasaki, still riding his tiny fixed wheel. His fitness level rose.

After two months of that regimen, and running stadium steps with ankle weights, Finely felt ready.

He mounted his new bicycle, symbolically white for purity, and fat-tubed, for whatever you think, and set out for Carr-Painter's favorite roads. Eventually he saw her, riding toward him on a narrow lane. By the time he got turned around, she had at least a 100-meter lead. Finely put his head down.

He chased for miles, gaining on descents and long flats, losing a little on climbs. Just as he entered oxygen debt for what seemed the 20th time, he drew up next to the effortless-looking Carr-Painter.

He panted, "Excuse me, but if you have a few minutes, post-ride, and you could join me, perhaps, for an electrolyte-replacement cocktail, I could share some rather interesting ideas I have about product endorsement."

"Exactly what I had in mind," the red-headed beauty replied. "Your training camp, or mine?"

As everyone will know, Finely and Carr-Painter-Finely soon assumed their place as one of the world's most loved and admired royal couples. Life in Pelotonia quickly got its act back together.

The imposing pair retired to rustic Cannon-dale where the men are strong and handsome, the women are strong and pretty, and the welds are, well, just strong.

55

SO FAST, PART ONE

TONY SAID he wondered if guys had really gone so fast in the old days, like when Bob was riding.

"There were so few bike racers then," he went on, "maybe you didn't have to be so good to do okay."

"Racing is racing," someone else said. "Those guys wanted to win just as badly as guys do today. I'll bet he had to be *really* good to get his picture on posters and all."

All us bikies, and even some of the not-so-committed regular customers at Bob's shop, knew Bob had had a fairly successful career racing on Chicago-area tracks 20 years ago. Now, he clearly knew everything there was to know about a bicycle, but he never gave us a peek at anything like athletic prowess. He rode his old track bike on errands and once in a while he took short rides in the country. Still, no one saw him do anything you could call high-performance cycling.

Now and again, someone like young Tony would bring up the subject of Bob's ancient speed, always out of Bob's hearing. Would he ever be fast again? Do the legs remember? We decided that they sort of remember, but not very well.

Bob's waistline definitely had forgotten its youthful dimension. A bike rider, though, couldn't help but notice his legs. They remained scarred, muscular evidence of the thousands of brutal board-track miles he'd ridden.

My guess is Bob started to get interested again about the time our club revived its old Wednesday night time trial series. We got good turnouts from the first at those "low-key" contests of speed. Naturally, all us racers showed up, but we were surprised to see dozens of seemingly less ambitious riders also appear. All the varieties of contestants behaved the same, it seemed to me. They acted cool and indifferent before and after each event, but they rode for blood.

Bob would hardly have noticed the advent of evening racing had not customers begun ordering expensive equipment, just for shaving seconds at those club events. He sold unprecedented numbers of parts he probably figured were useless, like alloy gear clusters and titanium rims.

He built sets of wheels with ridiculously low spoke counts. He began selling tires of exotic description and embarrassing price. He had to solve customer problems that never ordinarily needed solving. Like how to prevent chains from jumping off of single front chainrings without the weighty assistance of front derailleurs. Or how to place seven tiny cogs in the space where five larger ones had been.

Bob had to endure this mania while bombarded by continual war-storying about Wednesday night racing. Even so, half the summer passed before anyone noticed the slightest change in his habits.

First, I saw him pawing around in a box of old-fashioned inch-pitch cogs and chainwheels under his cluttered bench. Then, Andy told me that he and his girlfriend, peering in the shop window late one evening (Andy pointing out his dream bike), saw Bob making rubbing motions on some bicycle, as if he were polishing it.

Billy was first to report he'd seen Bob out on the road all alone, early on a weekday morning. But Billy was not the last. As sightings got more frequent, it became obvious that Bob was actually training.

Two or three of us, who felt sufficiently in favor, tried to get Bob to comment on his intentions. Would he like company on his rides? Did he feel some of the old form returning? Would he show up at the time trial some Wednesday night? He deftly evaded all our questions.

Alan told me he'd seen Bob out on the time trial course itself. He saw Bob ride in one direction, then the other, as if testing himself under race conditions. That same week, I saw him leaning on his bench just after closing the store, gazing at an old grease-stained gear chart.

Now, the fates of nations may not hang on these little dramas, but take it from me, we got excited. We watched without saying anything, noting each centimeter lost from Bob's waistline. We silently applauded when his trimmer middle forced him to take a new pair of shorts from his stock.

Every club-race night we dared to look for Bob at the start. Finally one Wednesday toward the end of August he slipped up to the table and signed up just before entries closed. I watched him rolling around, warming up on that old track bicycle, nodding to customers and to us hangers-on, not saying much.

He had on his ancient racing shoes, the ones with leather cleats tacked to the soles, and his old cracked leather racing helmet. The shoes showed unmistakable signs of a recent shine. The paint that remained on his old track iron gleamed. His legs, though, someone noted, remained unshaved.

I'd signed up and ridden early, so I'd finished my race when Bob took off. I watched as he wrenched at his bars and stomped powerfully on the pedals, muscling the bike's high, single gear. A cheer went up from the small group of us at the start/finish.

I can tell you the course is not nearly flat. I assume Bob suffered terribly heaving that big gear over the four or five steep rollers out there. And lots of guys thought it was blowing harder than usual after the turnaround that evening.

Whatever the reason, despite his ambitions, despite our hopes for him, our leader did not finish in the top third that night. Nor, to be honest, did he finish in the third below that. He did turn in a creditable time, a time only 14 seconds slower than that of Steve Riley's wife, Barb.

And Barb, we agreed unanimously, rode remarkably well. Amazingly well, we thought, for a woman in her fifth month of pregnancy.

SO FAST, PART TWO

IT LOOKED like Bob had lost a key ingredient for success in our club time trials. Though stylish, he lacked speed. Speed, a frequently used word among cyclists, can mean many things. Whatever you meant when you used that word, Bob lacked it.

After his none-too-successful debut, old trackie Bob quit showing up at our Wednesday evening events. He persisted in training, though. We'd see him, out early in the mornings or just before sundown, spinning on that old track iron, smooth in his low fixed gear. Smooth, but not very fast.

At that time, interest all over the country in veterans' racing began to increase. Veterans' racing, we thought, what a novel idea: guys over 40 slugging it out, just like kids, in road races and criteriums, risking coronaries and debilitating injuries. We racers thought that was terrific. Guys we figured were scuffing their feet on death's doormat turning out to race their bikes just like we did.

We joked about a Geritol Grand Prix and road races that would have to be timed with a calendar. We chuckled at the idea of follow cars equipped with spare wheels and cardiac care. Bob continued to train and did not chuckle.

When a well-to-do customer traded in a perfectly clean five-year-old Italian road bike on a new one, wanting the "latest thing," Bob set the trade-in aside and discouraged potential buyers. After a while, we realized he had quietly acquired a modern derailleur bicycle.

He kept on riding the fixed gear on training rides and on his errands. I think he began riding the bike more and driving his old pickup less. We noticed all that but said nothing; after his effort at the time trial fell short, we felt the less attention, the better.

Bob rode through the winter, except when it rained. He took his old bike home with him in the pickup in bad weather. We thought he might have a set of rollers at the house, but no one asked. He didn't gain weight over the winter months, and he ate as many cheeseburgers from the diner up the block as ever. He must have been doing something right.

By late February, he was piling up the miles, still entirely on the stiff-hub bike. His face showed color, and his eyes gleamed. He'd lost the last vestiges of waistline pad. His thigh muscles always had looked stupendous, relics of his six-day-racing successes. Now they looked a little less bulky, more defined.

First of March Bob started riding the 10-speed. When we saw him, he'd be spinning in gears as low as ever—slowish, spinning miles. The third week of March he showed up for one of our group rides. On the road, he neither slowed us up nor set the pace. He took average pulls and pedaled silky smooth.

We all could see how well he sat the bike and how easily he made it go. We had no idea if he had developed any speed. He rode with us about once a week, never aggressive but never off the pace. He seemed to float along, but if a gap opened he could close it almost instantly, showing no effort at all.

Around the shop, Bob didn't change a bit. He endured us racers and treated cycling newcomers with incredible patience. Bike shops, to be honest, were not nearly so busy then. Employees had time to show people how to fix flats and to speak to them about bicycle safety. Bob made sure he never got so busy he couldn't do those things.

In the springtime, we racers focused our ambitions on a road race promoted by the local tourist club, run traditionally in late April. That year, the club added a veterans' event. The vets had to ride 40 miles, same as the juniors. The hardest part of that course is a steep climb about two miles long, just past half-way through.

Since the course was close to home, we'd try to train on those roads once or twice the week before the event. It was on one of those prerace rides that I saw Bob, grinding up the hill as I flew by on my way down. I waved, but we passed each other too quickly to speak. I knew immediately that he intended to ride the road race.

That thought made me worry. He'd done so poorly at the time trial. What if he trained and rode modern equipment and *still* couldn't cut it? Then, 10 days before the event, Bob fell off his bike.

He'd been in a paceline on a club ride. A new rider three guys up saw a dog and braked suddenly. Bikes and riders covered the road. Bob didn't fall hard, but he lost some skin and bruised his knee. I wondered if he'd still try to race.

As I drove out race-day morning, I saw Bob, in his warm-ups, pedaling to the start. I waved and looked in my mirror, trying to see if he was favoring his knee. At the shop, I'd noticed it was still swollen, but whether Bob's knee was painful or not, nothing visibly spoiled that spin. I crossed my fingers.

I got busy with my own race while they ran off Bob's, so everything I can tell you is hearsay, but it's probably accurate. The vets' race started off pretty fast but soon slowed, as the nervous guys realized they weren't dropping anyone. The climb promised to split everything up soon enough.

Bob mostly sat in, is what I heard, and took a couple of pulls. I suppose he must have felt kind of good, back in the pack after all those years. It must have been sort of soothing, sitting in the group on those lightly traveled country roads, once the pace settled down. The hill remained, though, the big problem.

This part is good and bad. Bob had some sour luck, but at the best possible time. His front tire blew out its sidewall, scaring some of the guys. No one fell, and Bob got over to the shoulder safely. The senior pack had just passed the vet group. Suddenly the senior support car appeared. A mechanic handed Bob a wheel.

He had probably lost only a quarter-mile to the pack, but the climb started barely a mile up the road. Bob tried to make up as much time as possible before the hill, according to the support guys, but the real story happened after the climb. It happened on the valley floor, on the slightly downhill curvy road, on the fast 15-mile stretch to the finish.

They say Bob passed five or six guys on the descent, guys who'd gotten sawed off on the climb. None of those men could stay on his wheel, not for any more than a few hundred yards. On the flat, they say, he turned the big gear as easily as he had the 63-incher he trained on. He gained steadily on the pack.

Bob caught one chaser after another, shedding each man off his wheel almost immediately. Three miles from the line, he made contact with the bunch, rode straight through to the front, and shared the pacesetting with three or four others.

Club members had the start/finish area closed curb to curb. A dozen veteran men appeared, spread across the road, to contest the sprint. Four of those men, as I understand it, pulled away from the rest. Bob pushed his wheel in front of the other three and held it there, sprinting like you'd think he would: impossibly low gear, legs spinning like a turbine, no waste, no visible effort. People screamed—a local hero, unbelievable.

After the finish, as near as I can find out, he picked up his warm-ups and kept on riding. While we waited for the other races to end, he must have pedaled home. Certainly he was nowhere to be found —unwilling, I guess, to be congratulated. At the roadside award ceremony, when the rep called Bob's name, I went up to collect the prize.

I gave him his prize at the store on Monday. He'd won a fine set of hubs, that anyone would've wanted. As it turned out, he had donated them himself. He must have felt funny about keeping them or selling them; that same week he strung them up into race wheels. He gave those wheels to a junior for whom he seemed to have less distaste than he had for the rest of us.

As far as I know, that kid is riding them today.

TIM'S DAD

TIM NEVER complained. He'd set out to become a bike racer and know all about bicycles. If learning about bikes meant emptying bike shop wastebaskets, that was just fine with him.

He worked for Bob all one summer. He loved riding his bike, and he loved listening to Bob's stories. He always got to work on time, and he listened to Bob without stopping what he was doing.

By the end of the summer he could build wheels and assemble professional bikes to Bob's satisfaction. And we had clean floors and empty wastebaskets until school started.

Tim never hurt himself around the shop that I can remember. I know he never fell off his bike hard enough to mention. I do remember thinking he was kind of accident-prone, maybe a little clumsy. He stumbled pretty often in his house, he told us, when we'd ask about a bruise or a swollen hand or a limp.

Bob had gone to school with Tim's mom, and he gave the kid a job at her request. I think Bob never knew Tim's father. He called Tim's mom by her first name, but I never heard the dad's name mentioned. Don't know it today.

We did learn a lot about the father, though, because Tim was so proud of him, spoke about him a lot, all in glowing terms. I remember thinking that was not really typical; it was great to hear a boy rave about his dad.

My own father never knew or understood anything until I got well beyond adolescence. Then he became remarkably aware and perceptive. Tim's father developed earlier, evidently. He and the boy did stuff together regularly. Tim claimed his dad was excited about bike racing and would show up all season to watch his boy ride.

Tim's dad never did drop by the shop. "He's just too busy," Tim said, and described some ambitious activity his father had undertaken. He also missed the year's first few races, just, Tim told us, from being so doggone busy and successful. He'd get there when the season warmed up and races got important, Tim said.

I was lacing a wheel when Tim came in with the black eye. He immediately set to work straightening up the store, just as if a sizable portion of his face were not bruised purple-black.

"Jeez, kid," I asked, "where'd you get a shiner like that?"

Tim said he'd stepped on a rake, the handle had got him. Bob saw the eye and asked Tim about it. He heard about the rake, too.

"Tim," Bob said, "is it true about the rake?"

Tim kept cleaning the workbench as if he hadn't heard.

Bob said, "Wait a minute, Tim. Look at me. Is it true about the rake?"

"Sure it is, Bob," the kid said. "Why are you so suspicious?" Bob asked Tim, was he having trouble with his father?

"My father? My father?" the kid asked. "Are you kidding? We get along great. Hey, can I get back to work now?"

Bob never said a word about the eye again. If the kid showed some evidence of injury when he came to work, well, that was Tim's business and not his. Tim's mom came by one day, and she and Bob went to coffee down the street, but Bob was gone only a few minutes. He never said anything about the visit.

Tim rode with us in the mornings all summer. He was serious on the bike, a hard rider. If the pack dawdled, he did catch-up sprints, dropping back, then bridging up to the group.

He seemed to understand the subtleties of bike racing as if he'd always known them. He could sprint in a straight line, he could find shelter in a crosswind, and he could fit right in a paceline of any variety.

He had the horsepower to make other guys his age hurt. But he never hammered anyone on training rides and never strung out a group or misbehaved at all. At races, though, he was tough. Tim didn't always win but, if you beat him, you earned the victory. By June he was one of the two or three best juniors in the district. Still, his father had not come to a race.

Fact is, I never saw Tim's father until our club ran its annual criterium around Memorial Park downtown here. The junior race was next-to-last on the program, right before my event. I was rolling around, warming up, through most of Tim's race, but I saw the finish.

Tim spent the whole race at the front, I heard, working with a few others. The idea was to keep the pace so hot the weaker riders couldn't rest. By the last lap, Tim and another strong junior had broken away from the remains of the pack.

The two of them had a half-lap on the field. They rode fast enough not to get caught but not wide open, watching each other in wary anticipation of the sprint. I knew Tim especially wanted to win this race, his hometown criterium. I yelled, "Tim! Tim!" and pedaled over as close to the finish line as I could.

They started the sprint side by side. Just before they crossed the line their handlebars tangled, the bikes lurched for an instant, and both riders were thrown to the ground.

Tim got to his feet before the other kid. He stood there shaking, red faced, screaming at his rival. Then Tim pulled the other kid to his feet and began punching him in the face, in the chest, in the face.

For that moment we all stood paralyzed, I guess. I stayed where I was, dumbly holding my bike. I saw a man run from the crowd, his face contorted in pain at what he saw. I watched him run to Tim, yelling Tim's name and begging him to stop, grabbing Tim and pinning down his arms, dragging Tim away from the battered racer.

I saw the man put Tim up against a tree and sit under the tree at Tim's feet and cry. I watched them until I remembered I had my own race to ride. I rolled away down Prospect Street.

I don't understand everything about Tim and his dad. I do know that the kid worked the rest of the summer for Bob and did his job and never, ever complained. For that time, the rest of that summer, which is all I know about, the kid seemed to have lost his clumsiness.

I know for sure he didn't step on any damn rakes.

BEFORE THE RACE

HE STARTED taping at the bottom of the left handlebar. He concentrated on wrapping the tape tight and even. Later his jaw would ache from clenching his teeth while he worked.

He liked the clean white tape before a race. It was a nuisance to wrap the bars so often, but it had become part of his prerace routine. He liked the fragile newness of the white cotton. He liked how the bars stuck to his hands on the starting line.

He folded the brown rubber brake hood out of the way and wrapped underneath. He imagined himself at the race, warming up. He saw himself grinning and joking with the guys. He could feel himself there in the late morning sun, his tense muscles loosening, soothed by the familiar motions of pedaling.

He pictured himself on the line, calm and ready—more than ready, eager—for the start. He saw himself straddling his bike, one foot already strapped in tight. He saw himself leaning over the bars, forearms resting on the tops, coiled but cool.

He taped up to the engraved, thick section of the bar, cotton smoothly meeting aluminum at the shoulder. He finished the left side with a turn and a half of plastic tape that matched his frame. The left side of his bike looked so professional he had to smile.

The second half always went faster. As he began wrapping, he again imagined himself on the starting line, as he would be in the morning. He felt his own poise, his readiness, and the unease of his opponents. They were jittery, almost unable to stand still and wait for the start. One circled behind the group, too nervous to stay in place. Another absently clicked his brakes. Several, he noted, had dirty tape.

The dirty-tape image surprised him, made him smile. He thought about the first time he'd tried the fresh tape before a race. He'd decided to retape at the last moment, after completing the rest of his preparation.

His hands had been so grease-stained and soiled with tire glue and chain lube, there'd been no saving the new tape from gray.

That was one of the things you learned, he thought. Like how to get away from the line in a criterium like the one tomorrow, without crashing or getting hit by someone else. Like how to get your foot into a toeclip in a hurry without missing and whacking your shin with the pedal. Like how to cope with the speed of the first lap, the shock, how not to be intimidated.

He thought about that first lap. He felt himself starting, surging forward at the gun, in the perfect gear. His foot found the clip by instinct. He saw the first corner getting close. He saw himself and three other men, shoulder to shoulder, setting the pace for a hungry pack.

He wrapped the top of the bar, careful to avoid wrinkling the new tape. He'd be on the bottoms tomorrow, though, he thought, on the hooks, low on the bike, to pass cleanly through the air at racing speed. He could feel how his back would be bent, his elbows flexed, as his legs rolled the big gear around.

He and three or four other men, he imagined, sharing the work at the front. Working. While other men, thinking themselves clever, sat behind and waited.

Working together, smooth and powerful, opponents to be sure, but allied in the task at hand. Keep the race speed high, get rid of the unfit, discourage the sleigh-riders, the wheel-suckers.

As he taped around the right brake lever, he thought he could feel the race speed. He heard the sound of silk tires singing on the road. He heard the wind howl in the straps of his helmet. He heard guys grumbling behind him, back in the pack. Guys telling other guys to ride a straight line or to stay off the goddam brakes.

Those guys, though, those guys didn't matter, really. Just the front runners mattered. Front runners knew that riding a bicycle race amounted to more than saving yourself for 25 miles so you could charge hard for 250 meters.

One of those guys might beat him tomorrow, he thought. But that man would never earn the respect the pacemakers did. Not, at least, from him.

He cut the tape so the cut end hid under the bar. He added the last loop of plastic color. He assessed his work; the bike looked great.

He thought then of the energy of the pack, how it would build and fade, how fierce it got the last laps. He could feel the frenzy in his blood, as if he rode those last laps now and not tomorrow.

He could feel the frenzy, and he could see the last corner. He could feel himself in the corner, pedaling through it, smooth, elbow to elbow with two guys he'd never met, whom he'd probably like, and whom he desperately wanted to beat.

He felt himself rise out of the saddle to roll up the big gear. He felt himself spin the gear out and sit down, holding, accelerating steady to the line: a wheel, no, half a wheel, in front.

He stood over his bike, alone in his garage, hands on the drops.

He held the bars tight, feeling himself crossing the line, first across the line. First, by centimeters. Sure enough, even though his palms were sweating, when he lifted his arms in celebration, the new white tape stuck to his hands.

"Tomorrow," he said out loud. "Tomorrow."

COORS '88

I NOTICED Glenn Sanders leaning on the corner of a building watching the Reno Criterium stage of the Coors Classic. The last time I'd seen Sanders he'd been on his bike, placed about fifth overall in the Classic, looking smooth and in control. But here he was, out of the race.

He'd had some bad luck, he said. He'd gotten a blister on his heel, maybe from some new shoes he'd been given just before the Coors. The blister went unnoticed, as a minor pain can in the major suffering of bike racing. But the blister infected and swelled; soon the swelling spread to his tendon. The pain became inescapable. The leg needed rest, not more mountain stages. The war was over for Sanders.

Luck plays a big part in a racer's life, according to Sanders. He said he was beginning to have fun this season, no longer just hanging on trying not to lose major time, but attacking, making himself a factor in the races. Suddenly, the tendinitis did him in. Bad luck. You get used to it, he said, if you race for a long time. Sanders has been racing since he was 12 or 13.

"Probably you get philosophical," I suggested.

Sanders smiled. He said you get used to a feeling of helplessness. Stuff happens, he explained, like sickness, injuries, and crashes. You have good years and bad years. I looked at him standing there in his warm-ups; it was hard to believe he'd been so fit and competitive yesterday and couldn't ride his bike today.

Sanders said he thought he'd stay with his team for a while longer to help out the mechanic. Then he intended to go home and do things in his lab and maybe build himself a frame. He had friends who'd loan him a torch and tools. He said he felt like working with his hands.

We watched the racers, and Sanders said they all looked tired. He said that Alex Stieda, who had just taken over the general classification lead, seemed less tired than most and might hang on to the jersey. We got to talking about the new generation of riders, the Scott McKinleys, the Gavin O'Gradys. Sanders said those guys had incredible talent, incredible "hit," or power.

Those guys, '80s-generation racers, came up differently, Sanders said. People who began in the '60s and '70s thought of bike racing as a healthy, exciting, off-beat hobby, not a way to make a living. Greg LeMond, the exception, looked at bike racing as a profession from the beginning and made the right moves. Sanders said these young guys have been raised with the '80s emphasis on achievement and career goals, much the way LeMond was raised, probably.

Sanders said he expects that in just a few years we'll have 20 or 30 bike racers in this country with Ron Kiefel talent, Davis Phinney talent. He said a guy like Gavin O'Grady might do a super ride, as O'Grady did in winning the Santa Rosa Coastal stage a couple of days previously, just feeling good, riding a little over his level. Soon, though, the guy like O'Grady might find himself able to do rides like that routinely. With luck, of course.

As we talked of earlier generations of racers, Sanders mentioned that George Mount might have had a totally different career if he'd had more of an achievement orientation. Thinking about Mount, an outspoken, "personality" rider, got us to thinking about Alexi Grewal, Sanders's Crest teammate, another "personality" racer. We agreed that Grewal was the wild card in the '88 Coors Classic deck, that he remained perhaps the only threat to the 7-Eleven team's dominance.

I thought about how before the races, if you walked around the area where the team cars were parked, you saw two or three people getting autographs at the Crest car, maybe the same number at the

Wheaties-Schwinn car, the same again at the U.S. Olympic Team car. And you saw 75 fans clustered around the 7-Eleven car waiting for Andy Hampsten's autograph or to shake hands with Davis or Bob Roll or Ron.

Now I *like* Davis and Ron and Bob and Alex and all the slurpies. They've earned the attention, to be sure, but hey, all those other guys ride hard too. Coors Classic hills are just as long and steep for them.

The only non-slurpie racer who gets 7-Eleven-style attention is Alexi Grewal. He's certainly not my hero, but I'm glad he's here. It's not good for *anybody* to have one team ride easily away at the U.S.'s greatest race. Grewal provides welcome tension and controversy.

Unlike most of us, Grewal has no heroes on the 7-Eleven team and would like to whup them as dramatically as he can. Also unlike most of us, when he is at his occasional best, he can do things impossible for mortal man to do. He can beat Steve Bauer in a two-up sprint, for instance. Alexi Grewal, the black knight with the skinny legs.... Sometimes it's hard to know who to root for.

The Sunday before the Coors started, three of us local vet riders took the Crest team for a ride in the East Bay, across from San Francisco. They'd wanted to roll around, get their legs going, maybe just for an hour and a half. During that ride, we led them up and down a couple of hills. Naturally, without trying, they hurt us on the uphills. We weakened and drifted off the back of the group. They chatted, sitting on their saddles, effortless.

But we'd expected *that*. The descents, though, were a surprise. We have steep, twisty, rough, nasty descents here, on which a familiar rider has a real advantage. We were the familiar riders; the Crest guys had never seen those roads before. Well, the long and short of it is: I couldn't hold on. Those guys ride their bikes so well, so naturally, they can descend so fast on unfamiliar roads.... It's amazing.

I mentioned to Glenn Sanders that I'd been unable to match their downhill pace on our little ride. He said the athletic ability of the riders is hard to appreciate. The level of skill isn't as visible to the spectator as the sheer effort and speed. Sanders smiled again and singled out Irishman Alan McCormack as a super bike-handler. He can do a U-turn at 40 mph, Sanders said.

I said something about how he must be disappointed to have had to quit the race. Sanders admitted he was disappointed but said he'd learned to expect setbacks now and again. I thought, "Gee, this guy is professional." Like lots of riders these days, he seemed calm to me, emotionally controlled, more so than the wild men of the past. I said so, and Sanders smiled.

"Not on the bike," he said, "not always." A really successful racer has to have a fierce aggressive aspect to his personality, but many times it'll only surface during races, especially when the pain level is high. Good racers, he said, tend to be pretty intense emotionally. In fact, he knew stories about certain calm guys who weren't always all that calm.

He told me about how he'd gotten confused in a feed zone during a hard race, how he'd thought it was a neutral feed. He'd grabbed a feed bag that turned out to be intended for another racer, one who should perhaps remain unnamed here, but who has won an Italian national tour. The unnamed racer, usually a model of mellow propriety, screamed at Sanders in anger. Sanders said for a few seconds he entertained thoughts of decking the guy. The moment passed, though, and both raced happily ever after.

Remember, you read it here: the placid-exteriored athlete you admire, that easy-going model of decorum, probably bares his canines now and again when the blood oxygen gets scarce. Even Glenn Sanders, the kind of guy you'd want your sister to get interested in, flashes his fangs at times. But you'll be able to see that for yourself, at the bike races, pretty soon when his tendon gets better. And something else you'll notice: no tartar on *those* teeth.

JUST A
QUICK QUESTION

"I'D LIKE to buy a bicycle. For getting in shape. I'm thinking about racing, someday, or maybe triathlons. Mainly, though, I'd use it for riding in the hills, on the back roads. And for occasional trips.

"I'd like easy maintenance. I'm torn between sealed bearings, sealed-bearing mechanisms, and the tried-and-true conventional setup.

"I haven't decided whether to opt for Italian craftsmanship and tradition or Japanese high-tech engineering. Or maybe French exclusivity.

"Oh, about my frame size. I know my *right* size is 58 centimeters, but I've had back trouble. I'm used to a 62, and I like it. Is the size all that critical? If I get a 62, will it be less stiff, built with the tubing I'm considering? Should we talk about the tubing? Shouldn't a 62 be plenty stiff enough even if my real size is a 58?

"If I can get answers to these kinds of preliminary questions, I can get on to the tough stuff. Like crank length; boy, I've pondered 172.5 and 175, and frankly I'm stumped. What do you think?

"I will say that I've always been a vertical-dropout kinda guy, you

'Would I be better off with aluminum or a composite? What's your feeling about butted spokes? How many water bottles do you carry...?'

know. Still, my brother-in-law says that if the frame isn't built perfectly, the back wheel will fit crooked. Is that true?

"Where can I look for a frame that's perfect? A local builder? Do you think he'd have a few minutes to talk to me about frames? Sunday? Do you have his home phone?

"What's your personal feeling about butted spokes?

"Jeez, you know it's hard to get to the bottom of some of these problems. At the last shop I was in, I asked about some of these decisions I have to make, before I can start thinking about a new bike. After a while the counterperson sort of lost interest.

"Isn't helping perplexed customers what you people do? Isn't that why you're better than mail order?

"Tell me. Isn't Tortelli a big factory? Do they use an assembly line?

Does Mr. Tortelli hire all his nephews to assemble the team replica megabike?

"Would I be better off with an aluminum bike? Or a composite? How about time trialing? Really? One of those? Does it climb good?

"Is a Mandolini a good bike? I know you guys don't sell them, but you *must* know something about them. Well, sure, I know all bikes are pretty good, but Mandolinis have the new tubing with ribs inside like support socks. Isn't that better?

"The article I read said the new tubing was the greatest advance in bicycle technology since the banana got shaped for portability. What did that mean?

"How many water bottles do you carry? Do you go on long rides? Oh. That's not very far. Do you carry many tools?

"Is eye protection really necessary? Do you carry tinted lenses with holes for Strokely Galactic Battlestar Commander sunglasses? Do you sell the replacement sponge sweat pads for them? Mine gets all drippy and awful.

"Oh, one more quick question. Is a 73-degree head angle impossibly old-fashioned? Could a bike built with an angle like that ever be fast?

"Can you run a cadence wire through a frame? Even if the frame's aluminum?

"Hey, excuse me, but that's a perfectly good, high-thread-count, Kevlar-beaded-and-belted tire you're chewing on. What do you think about those? Should I ride clinchers? Honest?

"No, of course I wouldn't mind talking with someone else. It does seem late for you to be having your lunch, though. Thanks. 'Bye."

"Oh, yes, thank you, how are you? If you could spare a few minutes, perhaps I can get answers to a few more of my questions. I'd like to buy a bicycle...."

JACQUES

I JUST heard. Jacques Anquetil is dead, dead of stomach cancer at
53. At this point, there's no way to know if he suffered for months or
died shortly after he was diagnosed. Not that it matters exactly, how
it went. Fact is, handsome Jacques Anquetil is dead.

I hate it that he's dead. I hate it for him, that he didn't get to live his
gentleman-farmer, race-commentator life until he was so old even his
legend creaked. He looked, in recent photographs, like he was having
a good time. I would have wished him a good time that lasted longer,
as if it would've done any good.

I hate it for him that he died a young man, and I hate it for me.
Whenever someone like Anquetil, someone who rode so far and well
and kept himself so fit, dies, it becomes harder for me to sustain the
belief that if I only ride my bike, ride my bike and eat kinda smart,
ride my bike and sleep good and stay skinny, well, I'll by God live
forever.

Jacques Anquetil did not live forever. He didn't even live a long
time. I guess he lived longer than some people do, people who have
awful misfortunes or childhood illnesses or AIDS. But I don't think of
those people as health-minded, fitness-oriented individuals like us. We
aren't like those unlucky people; we're going to live forever.

I wonder if Anquetil thought he would live forever. I'll bet he didn't think of his cycling as a fitness activity. He probably thought of it as work. He may even have had secret fears that all that stress might shorten his life. Maybe if you just ride at the level you and I do, and not as hard as Anquetil, a five-time Tour de France winner, maybe then you'll live forever. Maybe then.

Losing a man like Anquetil gives me pause, you know? I see old, fat people in the street, cigarette ashes spilled down the fronts of their sweaters. I see men in bars I know are there every night, sad men smoking cigars and squinting through smoky, stale, low light at some equally unhappy woman six stools away. I see people who eat heavy food and drink lots of booze every day, and they're old and doing okay, and Jacques Anquetil is dead at 53.

Maybe we're wrong, we athletes. Maybe we get to choose what's important to us, just like other folks, and maybe being skinny and fit is gratifying to us like a prime rib and a couple of cocktails five times a week is gratifying to them, and none of it has a damn thing to do with how long we get to hang around here doing our personal number.

If that's so then we can do pretty much what we please, forget about cholesterol, smoke and drink, you name it, and it won't matter. If that's so, a lot of people are going to be disappointed: people whose personal lives have to be scheduled for time slots after the ride and before the workout and the swim, people who think that if they stay young-looking and thin and beautiful they'll be immortal, people who think that the only good week is a 400-mile week, people who think life is an individual time trial and who appear as if, while they're standing there talking to you, they can hear the timekeeper's watch ticking.

And people like me, too, people who feel their lifestyles are healthy and reasonable, who feel that compulsiveness is someone's desire to ride more miles then *they* do. People who think that red meat should be eaten in moderation but assume Ben and Jerry are high-consciousness New Englanders who sure as hell wouldn't put anything in that stuff that would hurt anybody, especially anybody who rides a couple hundred miles a week. Even if he ate it every day.

Jacques Anquetil liked to party. He was famous for it. He took things, too, and told his critics that he only did what his trusted doctor or trainer told him to do. We're too smart, us U.S. bikies, to go for that brand of self-deception. We're clean. That's why we're going to live and live 'til we're too old to care, and Anquetil, who fooled his body into winning five Tours and umpteen Grand Prix des Nations time trials, is dead.

Someday science will discover just what Jacques Anquetil did wrong, how he made the fatal lifestyle mistake that took him from us at a still vital 53. Until then, I suppose it'll be kind of a mystery. I think that until they do figure it out, I'm gonna keep on pretty much the way I have been, riding my bike and not gaining much weight, even in the winter. I might try, during the holidays, to moderate my eating and drinking. Right now I feel like I might just stay away from a lot of wine and French food, rich sauces, stuff like that.

I wish I could understand why so many things about life are so mysterious, why healthy people die young and some sick people hang on, enduring discomfort for years. I wish I could better deal with the idea that all that clean living and exercise could amount to nothing, not the feeblest barrier against disease and infirmity. I wish I didn't sense the undercurrent of desperation behind so much of what my friends and I do. I wish Jacques Anquetil were still alive.

OTIS

"SCAREDEST I ever was, was on the back of the tandem with that guy Otis," Jack said.

"Otis and his buddy had broken records on that bike all over the northern half of the state. They'd sign up for some century, leave last, and pass everyone. Take 'em maybe an hour and a half to ride the 100 miles, eat a Fig Newton, shower, and split an apple juice. They were known to be fast.

"Anyway, I would never have had a chance to ride on that bike if the buddy hadn't hurt his knee on some record attempt. That time, they had a guy driving a Corvette along to hand up food; they were trying to drop him. After 750 miles in the 57×13, Otis's buddy's knee starts bothering him. What a wimp, eh?

"So Otis has this tandem, The Bike That Made Him Famous, and he has no partner. Couple of times he says to me, 'Hey, Jack, let's go out on the tandem sometime.' When he'd say that, guys who overheard would laugh. I asked, 'What's so funny about Otis and me on that bike?' They told me, and I heard them, but I guess I wasn't *really* listening.

"What they said was, Otis liked to go fast. He liked to do other things, too, like eat food and spend time with women, but what he truly cared about was the going fast. He liked to go fast all the time, not like guys like you and me. We do it when we think we can get

'I thought that, if I asked him, Otis would slow down.'

away with it, without hospital visits and convalescence. Otis does it always. Always.

"Remember, I was not a new rider at the time. I had done things on a bicycle. I had ridden down steep hills and around corners, many of them sharp. While I admit I'm not known as a fearless descender, I can usually make the post-ride lunch before the waiter brings out the cigars and brandy.

"I thought—and this is where I made my mistake—that I'd probably do okay riding with Otis. I noted how free of scars Otis's legs were. I thought about how nice he is. I thought (and wrongness like this is seldom approached—someone on the *Titanic* was probably this wrong) that, if I asked him, Otis would slow down. Right.

"Came the day. We adjusted the bike to me and rolled out toward the coast. Not being able to steer or shift or control your fate felt strange, but it was kind of exciting. The power of the two of us on that thing was intoxicating, like driving a V-8 car after a puny four-cylinder. For a good while, maybe 10 or 15 miles, I thought I liked it.

"It began to dawn on me that I was where I shouldn't have been," Jack said, "when Otis neglected to brake before the left turn at the bottom of the hill in King's Point. We negotiated that corner at a speed I associate with factory aircraft testing.

"I was stunned speechless. My mind raced. I asked myself one question after another. What if a dog ran out? Or a child? What if a car backed out of a driveway? What if I couldn't control my bowels?

"I began to speak to Otis in a reasonable manner. I explained patiently to him that I was alarmed, that I had not thought to make peace with my maker, that I had composed no will. I tried, using understatement, to communicate my concern.

"'Hey, you'll be fine,' he said. I was not reassured. And soon (be still, my pounding heart), there were the mountains.

"Otis's tandem is a terrific machine," Jack explained. "It's a road-racing tandem, not a touring bike, so it doesn't have lots of brakes. Touring tandems have brakes on both rims and usually a hub brake in the back, brakes on the bottle-cages—brakes everywhere.

"Otis had two rim-brakes, Campy sidepulls, but Otis did not use them. He did not use them. My fear, already past the maximum limit of dread I can experience, began to increase.

"Those mountains to the west of here are not really so high. The peaks reach only about 2,500 feet, but sections of the roads are as twisty and steep as those featured in famous European races. Bicyclists with experience, cautious bicyclists, riding safe machines at safe speeds, can travel those roads in relative security.

"Otis, though, Otis disdained safe speeds and, even though his machine was equipped with capable, well-designed alloy sidepull brakes, *Otis would not use them.*

"My mind has drawn a curtain closed over many of the most painful memories of that ride," Jack said, "but one moment I can remember clearly. We were passing a van on a steep descent, on the way into a blind corner. (Otis passed cars as soon as he came up behind them, no matter what the circumstances.) I remember having trouble with my legs.

"Mind you, I wanted to get around that van and back in our own lane as badly as anyone on the planet wanted anything at that moment. It was urgently in my interest to pedal with all I had, but my legs would not work. They turned to rubber.

"I remember willing them to work, to roll the pedals around the way they had so many times before. They would not work. We were about two feet across the double yellow line, even with the van driver's door, when this silver Mercury appeared out of the fog, coming at us.

"It was one of those midsized Mercurys with the vertical grill, trying to look like a Bentley. While I know now that it was probably not any larger than a small motor home, it looked like the *Queen Mary* to me.

"I remember thinking, *When it's your time, it's your time.* Horns honked; the blood roared in my ears. My legs, my trained, toughened, shaved bicycle-racer legs: Jello.

"Well, obviously if I'm here today to tell the story, we did not get killed. Otis steered us through a 6-inch gap between the cars; 44-centimeter handlebars through a 6-inch gap.

"Now, nothing will ever scare me again. It's like measles: I've had fear, I'm not going to get it again. I'm immune, but I'm not crazy. Once in a while, Otis will ask me if I'm ready for another tandem ride. I tell him I have to wash my hair."

ROADIE

ONCE NOT so long ago, a Belgian bike racer named Eddy Merckx won lots of races in an area known as Europe. Merckx won long races and short races, flat races and hilly races, single-day and weeks-long races. He won time trials by himself and mass-start events with and without help.

People avidly followed the sport there in Europe. You could stand at a bar anywhere on the continent and raise your glass to toast the best in bicycle racing; everyone in the place knew you meant Eddy Merckx.

Eddy dined with the reigning King of Belgium. Meanwhile Merckx himself reigned as the king of athletes in Europe. He met the Pope. His name became identified with ruthlessly aggressive, man-eating, beat-'em-to-a-pulp racing. Newspaper writers called him The Cannibal. He was as renowned as a rock star. "Ed-dy, Ed-dy," fans chanted, "Ed-dy."

When he retired he set up a bike factory near Brussels, building professional frames and complete bikes. He sought out distribution in the U.S. and made several trips here to promote his products, both at trade shows and in bicycle retail stores. I first met him at one of those store visits.

I took about a dozen cycling caps, imprinted with the logo of the shop I worked in then, to the Merckx affair. Embarrassed, I put the hats in front of him where he sat, saying they were for the boys back at the shop, not knowing if he understood. He nodded, smiled, and signed all 12 hats. I still have mine, always will. I thought at the time about how many autographs the man must have already signed in his remarkable life and how gracefully he signed all those hats for me. *Class,* I thought.

Later, at bicycle industry trade shows, I got to see Eddy Merckx once or twice a year. You could feel his presence in a room, I thought, and I still think so. Merckx is not an ordinary man. Always, at those shows, I'd shake his hand and tell him how nice it was to see him, that I hoped his trip was successful and pleasant. He always thanked me, quiet-spoken, his English better and better. *Class,* I thought again.

At the trade show this last fall in Atlantic City, Merckx worked the booth of his U.S. importer, Gita Sport. Each day of the show, I'd see him there, shaking hands and looking great. Ed-dy himself, working the show in New Jersey, far from home and family, greeting bicycle dealers from the eastern U.S. Does he need to do this, I wondered. I can't imagine he needs the money; almost certainly he retired a wealthy man. But here he is, the man himself, The Cannibal, the name on the frame.

Walking across the hall floor with Rich Carlson, the editor of *Winning* magazine, I remarked on Merckx's unassuming style, his common touch. "He's the king," Carlson said, explaining that each time he'd spoken to Merckx or interviewed him, Merckx had always made time, always listened to the questions, always cooperated 100 percent. Hey, Carlson said again, he's the king. Absolutely. *What class,* I thought.

The show closed, and the three of us manning our booth went to dinner to give the convention center staff time to haul out the huge crates the booth fits into for shipping. Working these trade shows is tiring enough, but the assembly and disassembly of the booth takes hours, and I hate it. Through the whole show, I dread packing the booth back up.

Dread or not, there we were, back from dinner, loading our stuff back in the crates. I was not a happy camper. At a lull in the action, I walked to the restrooms. As I passed the Gita booth a two-tone purple Merckx bicycle with yellow trim caught my eye. Whoa, I thought, that bike is pretty. Still walking, I noticed a dark, strong-looking man in a sweaty Giordana T-shirt packing up the elements of the booth. Damn, I thought, that's Eddy Merckx.

I couldn't get over it. Imagine Bruce Springsteen helping the roadies pack up the show. Eddy Merckx, Superstar, seen wrapping stuff up, putting it in boxes, sweating in his T-shirt right here in Atlantic City.

I thought about bike clubs I've belonged to, clubs in which three or four of the members did all the work so the other 200 (including me) could ride. I thought about racers I'd known who wouldn't dream of taking a weekend off from their Cat III "career" to help their club run a century or a race, or just to take a ride with new cyclists, maybe teach them a little bit about riding their bikes.

I thought about how difficult it can be to inspire amateur racers to help their teammates, to sacrifice personal interest for a common goal. I thought about how riders will take and take from shops and sponsors and resist giving anything back in the way of time or consideration.

I looked again at Eddy Merckx, who's already proved who *he* is, who has met the Pope and the King. I watched as he bent over the side of the huge crate to load another piece of the Gita booth in there. Eddy Merckx, solid and dark and, at least to my mind, dramatically set apart from the run of cycling mankind, helping pack crates. Hey, he can't do it just for the money. He doesn't do it because he has to. Gita could find someone else to pack away parts.

He does it, I'll bet, because it never occurs to him not to. Like signing all the hats and taking the time to talk to dealers and to chat with Rich Carlson. Like not just thinking about how pleasant and easy he can make things for himself, especially since he's done so many incredible things already. Most people wouldn't blame him if he got on a plane right after the show and didn't help a bit with the grunt work. He's Ed-dy, after all.

I'm sure he has a sense of the magnitude of his achievements on the bike. Probably in quiet moments he savors memories of some of the victories, the five Tours de France, the seven Milan–San Remos, the Hour Record.... Probably he remembers moments when he rode away from top-rank professional cyclists, heroes of thousands of fans, and left them gasping in dismay and frustration.

Maybe now and then he remembers breaking away, finishing Tour stages alone, already so far ahead overall that the stage-winning margin hardly mattered, driven purely by his hunger to dominate.

Not *this* evening, though; no time to reminisce this evening. Ed-dy and the Gita guys had a booth to pack up and beautiful bicycles to wrap for shipping; the display had to be knocked down and put away. Ed-dy and the guys would finish up, all at the same time. They'd put the shipping labels on the crates. Then everyone could go home.

I wish you'd have been there and seen it. You couldn't mistake it. Class.

IN THE ROOM
OF THE HALF DREAM

DAVID PUT on a little burst of speed at the top of the hill. Not a serious burst, certainly not an attack; just a kick-up-his-heels little spurt because he was feeling so good.

He got in the big chainring and settled into a rhythm, waiting for the guys to catch up. No one appeared. He looked back over his shoulder; he had a 30-yard gap, just like that.

"What the hell?" he thought. He put his head down.

"Sure, it's early," he said to himself. "Sure, it's stupid. I'll never get away with it. Everyone's thinking what a stupid move this is, so maybe it's not so stupid after all. Maybe it has a chance. What the hell?"

He shifted up a tooth and reminded himself to relax his legs and pedal fluidly. He bent his back and found comfortable places for his hands on the handlebar drops. He decided not to look back.

"What happens back there, happens. Let 'em catch me," he thought.

David found a pedal cadence he liked and weighed his pluses and minuses.

"Little tailwind—that's good; means the pack's draft is not so helpful. It's early in the race—that's good; no one believes I can make it solo. Forty-five miles to go—that's *far*. Maybe *I* don't believe I can make it."

Still, no one came up to him. David drank a little water and watched a drop of sweat bounce off his frame. A motorcycle drew up next to him carrying a driver and a passenger with a pair of spare wheels, one in each hand.

David reached down and brushed off his tires with his fingertips.

"Don't flat now," he mused.

"You're doing pretty good," the motorcycle rider said, looking at his speedometer, then up at David. "Pretty good. Not good enough, though; they're catching you."

David pedaled a little faster and bent his back further. He felt his strength begin to be tested.

"This is getting hard now," he thought. He heard the motorcycle engine gain a few rpm, then the machine dropped back out of his sight. He was alone.

He thought about a film he'd seen showing a Danish pursuiter attempting the Hour Record. The translation from the original Danish had been clumsy. The narrator spoke of the Dane, shown endlessly lapping a velodrome, as a man in touch with his potential, with his guts. A man alone with his stomach.

David had only seconds alone with *his* stomach; the motorcycle was back.

"You're doing better," the driver said, yelling behind his plastic shield, "but not better enough. They're still closing—two guys and then the bunch."

"I need a little more," David thought. "Maybe just a half a mile an hour. I must have that much left somewhere."

He thought about the chasers and wiped sweat out of his eyes. He thought about how neat it would be to have someone to spell him. He thought how two guys working together should easily be able to catch one tired man.

He decided that they probably would catch him and drop him, but they would earn every inch. Every damn inch.

A wheel appeared next to him. He turned his head just enough to see that just one of the chasers had finally caught him. The man's face dripped sweat. His jersey was soaked. The wheel dropped out of David's vision. The rider sat in David's draft, breathing raggedly.

After a quarter-mile, David moved over, making room for the other guy to take a turn at the front. The man did not come through.

"Oh," thought David, "so that's how it'll be, you wanker lowlife. Sit in and come around me at the line, then. Come around if you can."

David listened to the man breathing. He thought about sitting comfortable on his bike, relaxing his legs, pedaling smooth circles. It got hard to keep his mind concentrating on those things. He heard the wind and the blood roaring in his ears.

He heard his left cleat squeaking on the pedal. As he rode, the sounds got quieter and quieter. His vision narrowed more and more. Soon he rode his bike into a silent tunnel.

He thought about how well his good racing wheels rolled on the road. He thought for an instant about how much it hurt to ride the bike mile after mile as hard as he could go.

He thought about people who never did anything as hard as they could. He couldn't imagine what their lives were like. He remembered how some men come home from work and wash up and go racing in the streets.

The motorcycle pulled up next to him briefly, the rider in a hurry. He yelled at David that he might just pull it off, but David did not hear.

He saw cars parked on both sides of the road, cars with racks and bikes and wheels on top. He saw lots of people standing in the road making room for him to pass through. He got his hands onto his brake levers just as he saw a car he thought he recognized. Someone grabbed him as he was about to fall over, stuck in a still-tight strap.

Later he found it difficult to remember his breakaway in any detail. He found that frustrating—he would have liked to have recorded the experience more accurately. Someone showed him photos of himself crossing the line alone, no pack and no chasers in sight. He was amazed when he saw that he'd finished with his arms raised in the traditional victory gesture.

He had no memory of any line, no memory of raising his arms. David looked at the picture of the man in his jersey, riding his bike, winning the road race in a once-in-a-lifetime solo break. He barely recognized him at all.

THE BIG RING

OUR LOCAL club consisted mostly of tourists. We liked that, because tourists would promote and work at bike races. We just wanted to ride 'em. Many of those tourists pedaled long miles just like us racers; though they didn't develop all the skills racers did, some of them sure got strong.

We got to talking about strong tourists one day down at Bob's shop. A powerful six-foot guy named Dave told this "Big Ring" story. A Big Ring tale describes someone's breach of training-ride ethics (at least according to the storyteller) and the revenge taken by the righteously indignant narrator. The stories got to be known as Big Ring tales because many of them feature the phrase, "and then I put it in the big ring." Followed, typically, by the storyteller's description of placing the offender's nose *right* in it. Here's Dave's story:

"Four of us went out the flats. It was a kind of gray day, a little windy. But it didn't look like rain, and I felt good. We weren't going too hard; we'd raced on Sunday and were gonna race again Saturday. None of us felt like anything but some loosening-up miles. That was just what we were doing.

"Ten miles out we passed a group of cyclists from the club. I waved, and one of us said hi. They'd spread across the whole lane in a rough formation. Several wore colored cotton shorts with lots of pockets; some had handlebar bags. They were unmistakably tourists. I recognized most of them from seeing them on the road, but one or two I didn't know.

"After we rolled by them, we continued in our single paceline, each guy pulling about a minute. When I'd taken my turn and pulled off, a guy I didn't know came through. He was thin and had a tan. He looked good on the bike, but he wore the telltale khaki shorts. I noticed he had a large black saddlebag hanging from the loops on the back of his seat.

"I nodded at the guy, and he smiled at me. He sat on the front of the line and picked up the pace, little by little. None of us had to change gear; you almost couldn't tell at first that it got faster. As I dropped back, Al and Tim glanced at me. I guess we all wondered how long it would take the guy to decide to quit and go back to his friends.

"As I slid in behind Al at the back of the line, I noticed the pace had picked up a bunch. No one pulled off after I did. The tourist just sat there on the front towing the four of us along. I could see him once in a while past the other guys. He didn't look like he was straining. He just kept rolling down the road.

"The five of us kept going faster, but the increase was deceptively gradual. I shifted up once, then twice, just starting to work hard enough so I noticed my breathing. I began sweating hard, even though it was cool out there. I began to wonder just who that fellow could be.

"I could hear Al breathing more and more raggedly in front of me. A gap started to open between him and Tony. I jumped to Tony's wheel and, just that quickly, Al was gone. And Tony wasn't pedaling all that smoothly. He was struggling to keep up on what was supposed to be a rest day. Then Tim swung out of the line, shaking his head, saying that was enough for him.

"Tony bridged the little gap up to Martin, but that effort took all he had, and he was gone. I looked past Martin and saw the tourist clearly for the first time. He looked like he was working, okay, but not thrashing around on the bike. He looked ready for more.

"He was riding a mustard-yellow Claud Butler. The bike had no

'Martin seemed like he was doing all right but when he looked back at me I could see the strain on his face.'

front derailleur and only one chainring. Except for the black canvas bag slung from the saddle, it was all business. Martin seemed like he was doing all right on the guy's wheel, but when he looked back at me, I could see the strain on his face.

"I kept to the curb side of Martin's wheel in case he blew up. Sure enough, he began dropping back, inch by inch, until he clearly was out of it. I jumped around him, feeling the effort myself, and there we were. 'Thee and me,' I said to myself. 'Ride me off your wheel, buddy; you'll know you had a workout.'

"I rode down on the drops, sitting on the front of my saddle. The road was not quite flat, slightly uphill, and the wind came over my right shoulder, not too strong. The guy rolled the gear along without visible effort. I couldn't get over how strong he was, pulling like that for miles without a break.

"I could just see the Danville city limit sign ahead. The road leveled out a little, and I got a breather for a few seconds before he shifted into his highest gear and began to hammer. I still had my secret weapon, the state of the gearing art, my as-yet-unused 13 cog.

"I jammed the lever forward to the stop with the heel of my hand, into the 13, my Armageddon gear. I charged for the city limit sign with every fraction of horsepower I had. I started to come around him on his downwind side about a hundred yards before the sign. I drew even with him so slowly I thought I might be riding into a wind tunnel.

"I beat him to the line by about six inches, I think. I know I had deprived myself totally of oxygen; I was nearly out of my head at the line.

"The tourist slowed down for just long enough to ask me, 'Scuse me, guv'nor, how far is it to Danville?'

"And possibly long enough to hear my croaked reply, 'I don't know, man, I'm not from around here.' "

JERRY

JERRY SAID he couldn't sleep.

"I can't sleep," he said, "sometimes until two or three o'clock in the morning. I read old bike magazines. I even read articles about stuff I'm totally not interested in, like touring in India or Indiana or someplace. Or torture tests of sealed-bearing jockey wheels.

"I read old race reports," he said, "just to see if they slipped and used my name. Not much chance of that happening, though. If I finished fifth, they'll print down to fourth, is what happens.

"Oh, and last night, I reread that article from last year on how to time trial. You remember, how you can relax one leg every so many revolutions; that's really useful. If I relax even a little, they'll have to clock me with a calendar.

"I sleep worst the nights before races. Not that I haven't ridden enough races to get over getting the jitters. I guess I haven't gotten over my crash. Oh, yeah, I fell on a training ride about a month ago. Put a big dent in my top tube. I thought you'd heard.

"This guy hit the brakes in front of me *so* hard, like he was trying to stop the whole sport of cycling. I've got no idea why he did that; I think some farmer in Nebraska or someplace chased a chicken out across a country road. This guy thought we should all slow down and ride safe, I guess.

"I hit the guy. I was airborne so long I thought they might charge me extra for my bike. Just before I de-biked and touched down, Andy hit me without so much as a greeting. He gave me this world-class bruise that is only now fading, allowing me to sit normally on wooden furniture.

"We were somewhat upset, Andrew and I. The gentleman whose abrupt braking procedure had precipitated our misfortune had not fallen. He had, in fact, felt my wheel hit his, he said. He felt sorry I'd been riding so close. I said I was, too.

"I rode the bike home, but I didn't get on it much for a week or so, until the worst of the soreness went away.

"It's not that I'm worried about crashing at the races," Jerry said. "I'm worried about crashing and not having Bonnie around. No, we haven't been spending too much time together lately. Well, really we haven't been together at all for a month or so.

"I guess I got too used to having her around. Now I worry about things like remembering to eat or to pack my cycling shoes or not to get hurt.

"I think she had her fill of the bikie life. Not that I'm so bad. Not, y'know, like some guys who keep their Chevelle engines in the den. Or that tourist who was down at Bob's complaining his wife didn't understand him; he'd heat a pan of grease on her stove to soak his chain. The house smelled so bad their old cat left for good.

"Bonnie took her cat with her when she left. I hated that animal when she was here. Once I caught it digging its claws into my NoAccount Wheelman jersey. Now I even miss the cat.

"Nobody knows me like Bonnie. She could spot signs of over-training before I could. Stuff like forgetting to shave, or clean up after myself or carry dinner dishes over to the sink. You know, the kind of lapses you experience from chronic low-level fatigue and post-peak athletic form.

"She didn't call after I crashed, but her girlfriend said she told Bonnie I'd fallen, and Bonnie was sympathetic. Judy said Bonnie was concerned about me and my equipment. 'I hope he didn't hurt his precious bicycle,' is what she said, according to Judy.

"It drains my energy to have to find rides to races every weekend,"

Jerry said. "Oh, yeah, the Datsun. That was her car. We used to take it all around. Like I say, I have to scrounge around for rides now, but I save the money I used to spend to put gas in that car. I figure I can use the $10 or $15 a month for laying in the store of silk tires I've been thinking about. Not that I begrudged her the money; she's the one bought me my racing wheels last Christmas.

"Well, she left pretty suddenly, really. I came home from a 100-miler, it was a Wednesday, and all her stuff was gone. I went to take a shower, is how I knew, and I couldn't find a towel. I looked in her closet and, sure enough, she'd split.

"She left me a note apologizing for leaving me without some stuff, like the towels, and the TV, and tableware. Said she was just taking what was hers.

"You know, she was with me so long she had bikie talk down cold. In her note she said she'd thought about leaving for a long time. She'd made a firm decision. She asked me not to try to get her back. 'Stay off my wheel,' she said.

"I don't know, though, if she's as sure as all that. I'm thinking about calling and asking her if she'd go with me to that stage race in Pleasantville next week. She could hand up a feed bag like no one else.

"Oh, you remember that copy of *King of Sports* I borrowed from you that time? I'm sorry I took so long to return it. Would you mind if I borrowed it again? I'm completely out of magazines, and I get really restless at night without something to read.

"The last few weeks," Jerry said, "I just can't sleep."

A JUNIOR

BOB NEVER sponsored racers out of his shop, but once in a while, he'd take a liking to some kid and help him a little. He'd make sure the kid had a first-class set of racing wheels, or he'd loan him his old pickup to drive to events. He was always available for advice, never for sympathy.

I remember Bob helped this one junior, a skinny kid about six feet tall who could climb like crazy and roll pretty good. A pleasant kid, the junior. He smiled and tried real hard. He looked you in the eyes when you spoke with him.

I thought the kid had to be at least district-class, maybe national-class. As I said, his climbing was not to be believed. He'd bought his bikes from Bob all along and he came to Bob for answers to his getting-started questions. The kid was almost just right.

He had junior problems. Because juniors are not fully formed in body, they ride shorter races than grown men; they're restricted to lower gears. Because juniors are not fully formed in mind and personality, they act like juniors.

This kid tended to neglect things, things that turned out to be crucial to his success in big events. He'd get over his disappointment quickly after doing poorly in these events. Those of us who'd helped him get so close remembered longer.

For example, the kid, an angel-of-the-mountains type, looked good for Nevada City, the bigtime hilly criterium in our area. The Nevada City course is brutal, either grinding uphill or screaming descent.

He got a great start, second or third into the two-stage turn at the bottom of the start/finish hill. He led the field at the top of the first climb. I believe he could have simply ridden away—he was that strong. At the bottom of the descent, he fell off his bicycle. He jumped off uninjured but out of the race.

When I looked at his bike, I could see the front wheel rim had broken. The front tire had rolled off the rim, either causing or as a result of the crash. The tire appeared to have been installed without glue, and the rim had very little residual glue on it. He'd been riding his own wheels in preference to Bob's. Bob's wheels, to which he'd have been welcome, were less convenient to pick up before the race.

None of us knew what to say. We knew, and you know, that there are some things in life that people *have* to do. You have to die, eventually. You have to pay taxes, and you have to glue your tires. Otherwise, evil will befall you.

Like a lot of young guys, the kid had a "no-big-thing" attitude. So he didn't win Nevada City. He had another year as a junior; he'd win next year. How upset can you get over a little rim cement? Many of us, who'd never had a sniff at a chance to win Nevada City, found it harder to remain casual about the phantom glue. The kid promised to do better.

All season, the kid and his clubmate split the victories, top riders in their class. The other kid was heavier, a far better sprinter and probably a little craftier than our hero. Their rivalry could drive the maturity right out of their adolescent minds.

At the district championships, our junior and a rider from another club broke away in the hills. They managed to get well up the road from the pack. Our hero's rival, back in the pack, saw that at best he was riding for third. He went to the far side of the road and jumped hard. He got away alone, chased the two-man break, and caught, exhausting himself doing it.

When he made contact, he sat on, pleading temporary tiredness. That infuriated our hero. Instead of the two of them, clubmates, working together to get rid of the third man, they began screaming at each other. The one accused his teammate of chasing him down. The other pointed out that now there were two of them in a three-man break.

Sure as early-season saddle sores, the sprinter recovered not far from the finish and jumped away to win. Our kid could easily have dumped the amazed third rider and had second place wrapped up. Instead, in anger and frustration at being beaten by his teammate, 30 yards before the line, in front of most of the civilized world, he whipped off his helmet and threw it to the ground.

That act earned him an instant disqualification from a surprised and justified official. His second place at the districts disappeared, and his trip to the nationals evaporated, at the drop of a hat, so to speak.

I saw the kid's father wrangling with the official. I walked over there to try to hear what argument the father might use to get the decision reversed. I heard the father tell the official it was criminal to deny such a talented kid his chance at national success. "Because of a momentary lapse," he said. "Imagine," he said to the ref, "the frustration, the heat of the moment, the kid's fierce competitive instinct."

The official refused to budge. The father grew angrier and angrier at his refusal to come around. Out of the corner of my eye I saw Bob, who'd also been listening, start to walk over to the little conference.

Bob and the ref spoke in short sentences, quietly. The ref brought out his rulebook. Bob read it over the ref's shoulder. Bob eventually made the man see that the rules left some room for interpretation; immediate disqualification was not necessarily called for. The ref relegated the kid to 14th, the last place that qualified for the nats. He also suspended the kid for 90 days, beginning right after the nationals.

By the time Bob and the ref got the decision finalized, the kid had gotten into his dad's car and gone home. He learned of his rescue over the phone. I'm sure he felt grateful. Bob, of course, never mentioned the matter again.

The season had mostly gone by, by then. We saw less and less of the kid around the shop. The next year, Bob helped a woman who was just starting racing. She wasn't a winner, but she had a great attitude. She remained cool at heated moments on and off the bike.

I remember she sent him a thank-you Christmas card after that season. I remember clearly that the card stayed stapled over Bob's bench for months.

OUR RIDES

THERE WAS a time when our club rides lost cohesion, when they routinely turned into ragged hammer-sessions. No one liked that kind of disorder or benefited from it, not even the guys who regularly dropped the rest of the group.

It seemed that when we had two or three cycling "elder statesmen" in our number the rides stuck together better, out of respect for those guys, I guess. Most people thought those men knew how things should be done, so riders would follow their example. They'd form double pacelines where there was enough shoulder, and single, disciplined lines where there wasn't.

When the respected riders came along, our group started at a gentle warm-up pace, then gradually picked up momentum. Sometimes we'd drop a rider or two on a climb, then pause so the stragglers could catch. When strong but undisciplined young men surged off the front, the group would let them go. Soon those guys learned that peer approval came from a quiet display of pack-riding skills, not head-down, big-gear showboating.

During the rides, you could see those group values in action, but it was hard to talk about them off the bike. You'd hear questions like "Isn't the hard solo effort the better workout?" and, "Isn't this ride going the speed of the slowest participant?" and, "Shouldn't I go hard if I'm feeling extra good today?" Questions like those are hard to answer.

A new rider could go to the shop where he traded and get answers to all sorts of cycling questions. He could become technically sophisticated simply by asking questions at the parts counter. He could find out how long the chain should be on a derailleur bicycle, how to wash wool clothing, and how to join a bike club. Someone knowledgeable could tell him about pedal cadence and position on the bike.

He would still not have a clue about negotiating fast downhill corners elbow to elbow in a pack.

At the chaotic time I mentioned, our looked-up-to riders were temporarily absent. One quit riding to work on his new house, and another left to race in the east. Our rides quickly deteriorated. Maybe a guy or two would slip through a light just before it turned red, then look back and see the distance "gained," and decide to try to stay away.

And maybe then a couple of other guys would give chase, and two or three more would take off after *them*. That would generally be enough to string out the whole group and ruin the ride. The people who hadn't chased or who hadn't even felt warmed up yet got discouraged at the sudden disappearance of their training ride. The escapees rode hard but raggedly and learned nothing. The chasers who caught learned nothing, and the chasers who didn't catch gave up in disgust and oxygen debt.

Numbers at the starts of the runs began to dwindle. People started to speak disparagingly of "the ride." Separate smaller groups sprung up, leaving 15 minutes earlier or later, or doing the ride route backwards. I heard the grumbling and saw the rides, which had gone on for years, falling apart.

I caught Bob right after closing at his shop. He nodded his head as I told him about our problems, as if he'd heard stories like them before. He said he'd do what he could.

Next morning Bob turned out in front of the shop for the ride. He counted the guys: only six.

"Six," Bob said. "We start with six; we finish with six."

Our club rides lost cohesion and routinely turned into ragged hammer-sessions.

That ride was a dream. We rode in a double line mostly, at the most even pace you could imagine. Twice, a guy rolled off the back on long uphill grades. Each time, Bob dropped back and towed him up to the group. Clearly, Bob was stronger than anyone else on the ride, but he used his strength to hold the ride together, not tear it apart.

The following day was better yet. One man brought a friend who had decided to give our rides another chance. That made seven. Bob counted but said nothing. The seven of us finished together.

At one point, the friend got dropped badly on a climb. Bob rolled back to him, put a hand on the back of the man's saddle, and pushed him up to the pack. Nobody'd ever helped the guy before. He raved about Bob. He said it was the first time he'd ever finished a training ride with the bunch.

The guy's gratitude and amazement touched me. I thought about how, in team sports, the casual observer gets impressed by the solo "hero" effort. The true aficionado prizes the unselfish labor of the *team* player, the athlete whose good day brings everyone up.

Sure enough, word got around about our remodeled rides. Numbers rose rapidly as we regained dropouts and added first timers. Bob spent most of his time with the new riders, explaining about smooth lines in corners and warning them about overlapping wheels.

One day a week he led us in pack intervals. Another day we'd sprint for city limit signs, then immediately reform into our accustomed double paceline—elbow to elbow, six-inch gaps, friends.

Bob rode with us until he felt sure the discipline had taken. Normally he preferred to ride after he closed his store in the evening or very early in the morning. When our racer returned from his campaign in the east, he happily dropped right into our training routine. He told us, his second day back, that some of the places where he'd stayed had crummy rides.

"It was every man for himself," he said, "nothing like this."

A RELAXED POSITION

"THEY AREN'T made by the people whose names are on 'em," Stu said. "Too many of those broke. Except for two or three teams, their bikes are made by small, unknown builders, so you can't get the same bike the pros ride even if you buy one that looks identical.

"What you *can* buy is the frame the pros rejected. Might break. Now these bikes *we* sell are made just like the ones the teams ride. That's what the designer told me. Getting one of these is the only way to make sure you're riding what you think you are. One of these here? No, this batch is all sold. I may have some soon I can sell, though; hard to say."

"Oh, wow," I said, "that's really something. When I bought my frame, I felt sure it was identical to the one Giancarlo Guacamole rode in the Giro. It looks just like the one in the poster.

"Come to think of it, though, on that hill right before we stopped for lunch on Saturday, I thought I could feel the bottom bracket twitch just a little. Maybe it's not a team-issue Turtelli after all. Jeez."

"Those pros are really strong," Stu said. "You probably don't need a frame that special. Even on the fastest club rides, even the trick frame and all the new aerodynamic stuff might not make any difference. Then again, you don't get much time to train, do you?"

"I don't," I said. "Plus, I'm almost 40 years old. Some of the guys I ride with are just kids, living at home. They've got nothing to do but ride all the time. It's a wonder I don't get dropped more than I do, especially on that whippy piece of pasta I'm riding."

"Hey, don't put that bike down," Stu said. "Plenty of riders would love to have it. Why, in Poland or South America...."

"Oh, yeah, but I need every break I can get."

"They don't have motors," some guy at the counter said. "You have to pedal 'em. Even if they're light and slip through the air like a straw, every one I ever saw you had to pedal."

The guy stood there absently toying with a box of the super-expensive titanium spoke nipples that time trialists use with bladed spokes to save weight. I asked him, didn't he think some bikes performed better than others.

"They don't perform at all," he said. "One with lighter wheels might roll and jump a little quicker, but the rest of this stuff is someone trying to sell you something you hope will make you better than you truly are.

"Performance," he went on, "comes from pushing on the pedals, not pushing money across bike shop counters."

I sensed I was talking with an expert.

"What do you think about Team Turtellis?" I asked.

"I don't know anything about Turtellis," he said. "Are they blue? I've been riding my same old bike for years. I guess I've stopped noticing the new models."

"Yeah, they're blue," I told him, "but they aren't the latest thing. Mine must be a year and a half old. The designers weren't even thinking about aerodynamics when they built mine. Times change so fast."

"You mean the new ones don't get harder to pedal when you go up hills?" he asked.

"Sure, they do," I said, but explained to him that the new equipment gives you a definite advantage.

"Then the teams with the new stuff must be winning all the classics and tours...."

"Well, no," I had to admit. "Not yet."

"They're evidently less fit than the guys on the old stuff."

"Well, no, at least I don't think they are," I said. "There must be some other reason. The strongest teams must be tied up in contracts to use the old equipment. You'd think, though, that pros would use whatever parts they thought would help them win."

"I believe they would," he said.

It struck me that the guy made sense. I felt a rush of appreciation for the athletic purity of our sport and the silliness of preoccupation with hardware. I flushed with a warm fondness for my old blue bike.

"You know, I'm kind of inspired by our conversation here," I said. "I've come to a new way of thinking. I'm gonna go home and roll around a few hours on my old Turtelli."

"Hey, all right," he said, still leaning on the counter, dribbling the spoke nipples from one hand to the other.

He must have made his decision just as I stepped out the front door. I heard him speak to Stu.

"I'll take 28," he said.

THE SWEATER

I THREW away my old blue cycling sweater yesterday. I had the thing so long I can't remember being without it. It wasn't the first jersey I owned. The first was a light-blue and white one I thought looked like Felice Gimondi's Bianchi team jersey. I gave that one away years ago, without a second thought. The sweater, though, was tougher.

I think that sweater was made as the top half of an old-fashioned Italian warm-up suit, one of the ones with pants that looked like pajama bottoms. No one bought those pants; if I think about them I feel sorry for all those rejected baggy warm-up bottoms. I wonder what became of them and hope they're doing all right, wherever they are.

The shop where I bought that sweater closed not much later. I remember it as kind of an unfocused shop, one you'd seldom find a reason to visit. My girlfriend had bought one of the sweaters there for $15, a bargain even in those days. I stepped right up.

The label, printed in Italian, couldn't be decoded. You couldn't tell if it was wool or synthetic or a blend. I treated it like wool for 10 years.

The full-length front zipper made that sweater easy to put on and take off. If the day got warm, you could unzip it part or all the way.

I was too classy a guy to wear a sweater as ratty as that.

Or you could take it off and twirl it by the sleeves and tie it around your waist. Perfect.

That girlfriend and I rode together a lot. I see us in my mind in matching blue sweaters, riding side by side (only when safe, of course) down foggy, wooded country roads. We looked alike, and I think we thought alike, then.

She and I rode centuries and group training rides. We took moderate-length tours together. She liked to wear a railroad engineer's hat. Me, I was learning to wear a cycling cap Saronni-style, down over the eyes in front, perched impossibly high in back. Saronni, that year, was still being driven to races by his mommy.

Eventually, even though I learned to wear the cap perfectly, the girlfriend departed. The sweater stayed on.

I recall once, on a late fall ride, I got caught in a cold rainstorm. I got soaked, but the sweater kept me warm. I remember wringing water out of it in a restaurant bathroom and having to drop it on the john floor for lack of a place to hang it while I dressed. It was still so wet, even after the wringing, that it flopped loudly when I dropped it on the tile. That's a warm sweater.

I remember it covered in frost down the arms and across the chest on those painfully chilly, clear mornings there are never enough of. I remember how the cuffs frayed after the first couple years but never got worse. I can remember the blue of it bright and the new smell still in it. That sweater was new then, and so was cycling. I had yet to discover I had limits.

In those days I felt it was important to wear clean, unworn cycling clothes. I saw that some people who'd been at it long enough to own old bike clothing wore their mended, tattered stuff with no embarrassment. Not me, though; no patched tights for me.

I thought that if I wore less-than-perfect jerseys, or shorts, or whatever, I would be considered casual or uncommitted to the sport.

Years passed and I was still riding. I got less impressed by emblems of dedication one could merely buy. I became more aware of subtle signals, like class on the bike, that earlier I might have missed while looking at some turkey's jersey.

I won't say I've let myself go completely and ride in rags. I did begin to lose interest in woolen (later Lycra) perfection. I came to find certain articles of clothing (and equipment) pleasantly familiar and effective. I didn't want a new whatever, thank you; I liked the old one just fine.

I liked that blue sweater especially fine, as you may have perceived. My new girlfriend found the hole in the twice-mended left shoulder too shabby, though. She asked me repeatedly not to wear it.

I explained to her about the old girlfriend and the rainstorm and the frosty mornings. I tried to recreate the sound my sweater made slapping the bathroom floor. She was relentless.

I was too classy a guy, she said, to wear a sweater as ratty as that. It was giving a bad impression. So I threw it away. Hey, it was for my own good.

ROAD RACE

YESTERDAY I rode my first road race in a couple of years, certainly the first one I've finished with the leaders for longer than I'd like to admit. Now that I'm over 45 I get to compete with guys my age and older instead of sometimes 10 years younger. So, suddenly, just yesterday, I could smell success in a bike race. I was a contender. Gee, it was fun.

The last few years, as I matured in the 35-45 class, I felt I was going backwards. I *was* going backwards. Now I'm able (or at least I was yesterday) to get in the break and vie for a placing. It's been years since I've had to think about sprint-finish tactics, but, thank goodness, I'm going to have to now. I gave away a place or two yesterday, but no more Mr. Nice Guy. You'll see.

Those last five or six years, as I got less and less competitive, I lost interest in my own racing. Getting up and driving to some remote place, paying a fee, all the hassles, only to get dropped early on...depressing. Hey, I could stay home and roll out my door to a group training ride any day. I got to feeling that racing only complicated my life, that I could train year-round without needing to be getting ready for anything. I'd forgotten.

I admire people who can keep showing up at the races when, almost inevitably, they'll be dropped again and again. Like some women, for instance, in areas where not enough show up to divide the class the way they're doing here in northern California. And Cat IIIs and IVs who may never upgrade because of modest talent or lack of time to train. And old guys like myself who could do okay against men their own age but who keep getting older as younger, faster guys up the ante in the class.

Yup, if you're one of those people who persist in spite of regularly having to time trial in all alone, you have my respect. I did not have your tenacity. Maybe now, though, I'm remembering what keeps you going back: I got an awful good feeling at the races yesterday.

I sure had terrific clarity of mind during that race. It felt great to be so focused. The only other time I have that same centered single-mindedness is when I'm writing these stories. Racing felt much more intense than even the fastest training ride with the boys. On a training ride, it seems to me, some people expect a smooth, conversational paceline. Some look for faster (but still social) miles. Others expect a sort of unscheduled bike race. Obviously, any of these attitudes can (and do—yes, they do) change midride and then change again. Clearly, a training ride can be a complicated place to be. A race is somewhat more elemental: every rider tacitly states he or she intends to finish in front of as many opponents as possible. Simple, huh?

I don't like to drop people on a training ride. I prefer to wait for out-of-shapers in most cases, even when I'm feeling pretty good and could hang with the leaders. I confess that I've not always enjoyed finishing what could've been a terrific fast ride, doodling along with some poor soul who'd been sick or hadn't trained. I did it, though, and I'm glad now, but it sure took a long time that day. On the other hand, dropping people in a race is morally acceptable, even admirable.

And, boy, after yesterday's race, after I stopped shaking and changed out of my cycling clothing—after I drank all that water and ate the 26 Fig Newtons—boy, then I felt great. The noise in my head retreated. Calmness ensued. Far out.

The guy I'd driven to the race with had had to ride more laps than I did, so I had maybe an hour to hang around waiting for him. I drifted around the parking area in my sleeveless undershirt, chatting with people and sunburning my pale, wimpy bikie shoulders. I could sense a pleasant, unfamiliar silence in my brain. Whatever usually preoccupies me and keeps me from 100-percent concentration on the moment had gone.

I felt myself listening intently to my friends and acquaintances the way I wish I could every day, really paying attention. Hey, I was a super guy there for an hour or so. You'd have liked me.

Fact is, I might have skipped the event entirely. I'd been uncertain about going, but I decided that if my friend Bobby Lee would go, I'd drive over with him. I had a hunch he'd be the perfect person to ride with to the bike races. He was perfect, in fact, but it didn't seem so at first. Took me two phone calls to talk him into going....

On the way to the race, Bobby moaned and wailed about how he'd been sick for several weeks. He complained that his legs weighed tons. He told me he'd tried to sprint a couple races back and described graphically how he'd been unable to whip around his old buddy, the 13. Even the 14 cog, he said, had felt *hea-vy*. He blew his nose.

He lamented that *his* class, men 35-45 years old, had to ride three hilly laps, about 65 miles, and he'd only once all season ridden that far. He ran me down a list of his flu symptoms. He told me how hard he'd been working. He sniffled.

Bobby admitted that when he'd turned 35 he'd thought racing with the geriatrics would be like easy money. Although he'd done generally well, he'd been surprised at how fast some of those old dudes could go. Driving to the race took us maybe an hour and 20 minutes, and he grumbled most of that time.

I guess I was chatting with someone at the moment Bobby's race ended. I saw him a few minutes later as he rolled into the parking lot after warming down.

"Bobby. How'd you do?" I asked him when he stopped next to me.

"I won," he said, looking right at me. "Now," he added, "I'll have to take your abuse all the way home."

Right.

ALLEZ, POU-POU

THERE ARE so many memories: the lovely Dutch towns, the bike races, the chocolate, the red-light alleyways in Amsterdam.... But you know all about that stuff. Shame on you about the alleys.

You know how cold and rainy the Benelux countries can be, and how hard the racing is, and how tough the racers must be. I don't know what I could add that would mean very much.

You might enjoy hearing, though, about a lucky meeting I had with a few men I'd heard about for years. I had lunch, in the south of Holland, with several reporters from a major Flemish daily newspaper. Those gentlemen had covered bicycle racing season after season. In fact, they had seen so many races that they felt little urgency to follow the Amstel Gold Race closely.

They preferred sitting in roadside cafes, drinking aperitifs and Dutch beer, telling bike-racing stories to starry-eyed visitors like myself. Over strong coffee we talked about U.S. cyclists in the U.S., U.S. cyclists in Europe, Mr. Reagan, Libya, and Amstel Gold contender Joop Zoetemelk.

Zoetemelk was fortunate enough to win last year's world championships, but, as someone remarked, he has finished second *so* many times.

Talk of Zoetemelk led to talk of Raymond Poulidor, who almost never won but was always "there." Surely, most of you remember stories about Poulidor. He rode in the slender shadow of Jacques Anquetil in his early career and later in the broader shadow of Eddy Merckx. Pou-Pou, as he was called, rode the Tour de France until he was 40, finishing second time after time.

"Never once, never once, did Poulidor wear the yellow jersey of leadership in the Tour," said the veteran reporter. "Never was he a leader on the road, not even for a short period during a stage, so that he could be said to be in yellow. Think of that: the man placed well in Tour after Tour but was denied even minor victory."

The Belgian newspaperman shook his head as he thought about Poulidor. He explained that fans perceived the French racer as a thoroughly human but unlucky man, forced by timing to strive against virtual immortals.

The people embraced Poulidor, loved him. The men who beat him again and again were indeed heroes of sport. Fans held them in awe, respected their class. But fans adored Poulidor.

Anquetil parlayed time trialing ability and tactical skill into five Tour de France victories. He won the French race of truth, the Grand Prix des Nations, again and again. Excitement shot through European crowds when he pedaled by.

Poulidor, in defeat, drove them wild.

Eddy Merckx could open a 50-meter gap on 10 cooperating men and hold that distance until the men had exhausted themselves and given up. He could win a mountain stage, a time trial prologue, or a field sprint. He rode away from Poulidor and everyone else at every race worth mentioning.

Today, fans gather around Merckx to ask for autographs. They mob Poulidor.

The newsman told me that he'd been in a crowd at a Tour stage a few years after both Merckx and Poulidor had retired. New *grands* had replaced them in the headlines. The fans that day stirred as Fignon, Hinault, Kelly, and the others rode by.

Then, in the entourage following the race, someone spotted Poulidor, barely visible in a car.

"It is Pou-Pou in the car!" he yelled. "Pou-Pou, Pou-Pou," the fans chanted. "Pou-Pou, Pou-Pou."

The veteran sports reporter shook his head again.

"The men who beat Poulidor," he said, "were like machines. They were so gifted. Their victories were often without drama, except perhaps the waiting to see how badly they would demolish their opponents.

"It was difficult for the enthusiast to identify with Eddy Merckx, The Cannibal, who could crush mere supermen at will. It was hard to imagine what it was like to be Jacques Anquetil, the master tactician, a man who won economically, almost surgically.

"Ah, but Poulidor," he said, "who suffered for all to see in vain pursuit on the climbs, who was there for the finish but just a little too slow, who could roll almost well enough to break away....

"There's a pain in being second," he went on, "that we can all sense. To be as close to victory as one can be, without having it, as close to fulfillment.

"Second is the worst place. Worse than third or fifth or 11th. Think about it. Poulidor had years of 'almost' and years of adulation. The adulation shows no sign of waning. Was it worth it? You decide," the reporter said.

Ah, Pou-Pou, I thought. *Allez*, Pou-Pou.

GIVEAWAY

I GUESS it had been there forever. I know it was already there in the basement, covered by an old tarp, when I first started to hang around Bob's shop. No one had disturbed the dust and cobwebs on it for years. It looked like the oldest racing bicycle in the world.

Not that it was all that ratty, really. The paint had faded, but you could still read the decals. The colors in the enameled Cinelli emblem on the head-tube had stayed vivid all that time. I was struck, when I first saw the bike, by the strange old-fashioned shapes of some of the parts: the gear changers, the rusty toeclips, and the waterbottle cages.

The handlebar cage was empty, but the one on the down-tube held an oxidized aluminum bottle with a cork stopper, like you'd see in old racing photos. All the bike's alloy parts had dulled and filmed over with age.

The cotton tape on the bars had lost its color and frayed above the brake levers. No one had fussed over that old bike for years.

Occasionally, after I started working at Bob's, my tasks took me down to the cellar. Naturally, I sneaked a curious look or two at the old Cinelli. When I asked Bob about it, he said it didn't belong to him; it was just stored down there. I should ignore it. After a while I forgot about it almost completely.

There was no reason to think about that old bike when Bob's

nephew Charlie began staying with Bob in the summers. Charlie was 16 or 17 when he started spending two months at Bob's house each year, helping out part-time in the shop.

At first, the shop was just a place for Charlie to work. He'd keep the store looking straight, and he'd sell parts when we got busy. Quiet times, he'd kind of stand around and stare out the window as if he wished he were someplace else.

Bob gave him a reasonably nice used bike to ride around. Charlie got from place to place on that bike, but he by no means seemed interested in bicycle riding. I don't know how he felt about us bikies, dressed funny and smelling like wet wool, but he was always pleasant, if a little distant. We were nice to him because he was generally okay and, after all, he was Bob's nephew.

Most of the year Charlie lived with his mom, Bob's sister, in a town smaller than ours an hour's drive away. Bob told me the boy had lost his father in a car accident when Charlie was just a kid. When I saw Charlie and his mom together, it seemed to me they didn't get along so well.

In fact, he didn't appear to be especially close to his uncle, if you ask me, or to anyone else. I wouldn't say he looked unhappy, but he kept to himself and watched what went on.

The second year he worked for Bob, Charlie had grown taller and more curious. He'd added a couple inches of height by magic during the school year, and he seemed more interested in us bike riders and in cycling.

He wanted to know how far we rode and how fast. He wanted to know if we raced all the time or did we just pedal along and look at the scenery. He asked me if we felt trapped, locked to our bikes by the toeclips and straps. A couple of times I saw him heft my bike, then his, then mine again, shaking his head.

He began riding more, spins around town at first, then longer trips on the country roads we trained on. Once our group met him on the road; he fell in with us, but took another route after a few miles. It was as if he didn't care if he rode with people or alone.

He still had no actual cycling clothes, even though Bob would have sold him anything he wanted at cost and let him work off the price.

Bob didn't act any different around Charlie than he did around the rest of us. He answered his nephew's questions carefully, but he didn't appear to be just jumping up and down over the kid's new interest in cycling. Bob was getting in lots of miles himself at that time, but he never, as far as I know, went out of his way to convince Charlie to join him on a ride.

Bob, too, kept mostly to himself and watched what was going on.

We began to see Charlie on his bike in the mornings, when we'd be out on our training rides. Sometimes he'd sit in a while and then drop out, or he'd start up a hill with us and not be able to keep up, and we wouldn't see him again. He invariably insisted afterward that he was glad we'd gone on, that he wouldn't have wanted us to wait for him and spoil our ride.

As the summer went on, it took longer and longer to drop Charlie. He still rode in cotton shorts and sneakers, but he kept that loaner bike immaculate. He raised and lowered the saddle and bars and adjusted the brake levers until he looked pretty good on his bike.

Soon he wasn't getting dropped at all. He became one of the boys, riding in the mornings and helping his uncle in the afternoons. He showed all the signs: his suntan was arms-and-legs-only and he had suspicious dark patches on the backs of his hands.

He began to take more time with Bob's customers, especially those who were just getting started in athletic cycling. Since his own knowledge was only a few weeks old, he could understand beginners' problems better than the rest of us.

Bob saw all this happening and supported the boy in his offhanded way. He sprung for a pair of cycling shoes for Charlie, sold him some shorts for half of cost, and gave him an old but not so worn jersey of his own.

He showed the boy how to wash wool clothes and how to shine the whole leather cycling shoe, sole and all. When it needed it, Bob would work on Charlie's bike while the boy watched. Mostly, after watching once, Charlie could do the repair himself the next time.

Late in July, Bob asked the boy and me to stay after closing on a Saturday night. He disappeared down in the basement for a moment, emerging with the old Cinelli on his shoulder. I thought, "Oh wow, he's going to give that bike to Charlie."

Bob stuck the bike in a repair stand and asked us if we felt like doing some restoration work. Sure we did, we said, and Bob handed us tools.

I took off the wheels, cut the spokes, and threw them and the old rims away. I repacked and polished the hubs and laced up two new rims, ready for Bob to true.

Bob took off the cranks, bottom bracket, and headset, cleaned the parts in solvent, and reinstalled everything.

Charlie removed the derailleurs, shift and brake levers, and brake calipers to clean and relube them. He polished the aluminum parts and rubbed down and waxed the frame.

He and I put on the changers, levers, brakes, and new cables. We taped the bars while Bob finished the wheels. Bob glued one tire; Charlie and I did the other.

Bob got out a tape measure, checked the bike Charlie had been riding, and set the Cinelli seat to the same height. We all three stood back and looked at the resurrected old bike. Bob asked Charlie if he'd like to ride it around the block, under the streetlights.

As the boy went out the door, Bob reminded him to be careful on the freshly glued tires.

"You're going to give that bike to him, aren't you?" I asked.

"I can't really do that," Bob said. "It's already his."

"I don't understand," I said.

"That bicycle's been his since he was five years old," Bob said. "That's his daddy's bike."

JUST LIKE NEW

YOU KNOW, I didn't always wear a bicycle helmet. I used to think that the people who needed helmets wore helmets, and because I hardly ever crashed, I didn't need one at all.

At the time of my conversion, I worked at a bike shop in San Francisco, commuting from my home in Marin County by bicycle. I found relatively peaceful, traffic-free routes to work in no time.

After I'd worked in that shop just a short while, my boss hired an English guy to fix bikes. His family owned a bicycle store in England, the guy said; he'd been riding since he was a kid. At that time, he must have been about 35.

He knew his way around bicycles, as a mechanic and as a rider, too. I'd seen him around for at least a year, in shops and out on the road. He'd always seemed sensible and genial to me. I suppose I thought of him as a casual friend.

He rode an English bike equipped in what I'd call the Brit Glamourless style. The frame was built of some Reynolds variant, the cranks were attached by cotters, the rims were steel, and the rear tire was one of the then-new knobby clinchers. A typical British saddle-bag, not a pannier but a single huge floppy bag, hung from his saddle. A cheap steel luggage rack supported that bag, preventing it from dragging on the tire. He used fenders year-round.

Do not think because his bike was undistinguished that he could not ride. He pedaled everywhere. You'd see him on top of Mount Tamalpais or on the Golden Gate Bridge. You'd see him riding alone or with a gaggle of Marin County tourist-types, mostly women, chatting amiably as they rode. His bike, you might notice, always weighed 10 pounds more than the next heaviest on the ride. His second day on the job, he asked me to ride back to Marin with him. Sure, I said, we'll cruise on home. I rode veteran's class races then and most of my friends were and are "performance" bikies. Still, I generally just pedal along on rides, and I am especially mellow when I commute.

Not him, though. As soon as we set off into the rush-hour traffic, I could tell he felt a lot more aggressive than I did, at least that day. He shot between cars to gain a few yards. He did skillful track stands at stops. He jumped across intersections as soon as the lights changed. He rode in a manner I thought was suicidal.

He would drop back a little on the steep hills, but everywhere else I had to strain to keep up. I thought, "Gee he takes a lot of chances." I nearly said something about how I really never rode that hard in the city, but I didn't. I just shook my head and tried to keep him in sight.

He rode spectacularly fast on the Golden Gate Bridge. He'd warn pedestrians with a handlebar-mounted bell just before he bored through groups of them flat out. He never slowed at all for the slippery bridge towers, rounding them blind at about 15 mph. "How can he ride like this day after day?" I asked myself.

Somehow we made it safely across the bridge. He'd gotten well warmed up by that time, so I had all I could do to stay on his wheel down the hill into Sausalito. As we came close to town, traffic began to slow. My friend did not.

At the second downhill turn, a blind right-hander, a line of cars had stopped. Without hesitating, he rode over to the center line to pass the four or five cars I could see. I thought he'd made a truly irresponsible move. I got on my brakes, waiting for the cars to start moving. No accident happened where I was.

The cars had stopped behind a Rabbit. The driver was waiting for a hole in oncoming traffic so she could turn left. My friend, on the center line, missed the oncoming cars but hit the turning Rabbit, bouncing off the front fender. The crash buckled both his wheels and threw him on his head in the street.

There was no way he could have avoided that collision once he'd committed to the pass. The street is narrow there; cars were everywhere, steel in every direction. As soon as I got over my disbelief—my refusal to believe the accident had happened at all—my stomach went queasy.

The woman in the Rabbit turned out to be a nurse. She got right to work mopping up blood around his face with paper towels someone brought from the nearest house. My friend lay there on his back in the street bleeding and asking for me. He asked me if I'd get his billfold out of the saddlebag and put it in his pocket. He told all the folks gathered around that he couldn't pay for medical help, he didn't have any money. He bled like mad from around his eyes and forehead.

I hated being there, and I felt ashamed of myself for hating it. I felt weak and disgusted at this horrible thing my friend, who had appeared to have good judgment, brought on himself. I had vivid "there but for the grace of God" flashes.

Police cars and an ambulance arrived. Paramedics jumped out of the ambulance and tended to my friend. While I stashed his bike behind a house and wrote down the occupant's name and address so my friend could get his bike back, the paramedics loaded him aboard. One of the paramedics approached me and asked my name. He said the injured man wanted to speak with me.

I forced myself to climb up into the ambulance. I looked at my friend stretched out there on the portable bed, head first in the van. I saw how his feet kicked up and down under the white covers the attendants had thrown over him. He wanted to know had I taken care of his bike. Sure, I said, the bike's fine.

The ambulance drove away; the police cars left. That corner became just a corner again. My own bike remained where I'd left it, leaning in someone's hedge. I looked at it and had no desire whatever to ride it. Reluctantly I climbed on, coasted down the hill into Sausalito, and called my girlfriend from the first phone booth. No answer; no one to pick me up. Detuned as I was, I had to pedal home.

I felt upset, filled with distaste the whole way home. For a couple of days I believe I was hard to live with. The evening of the accident, I called the emergency room. One of his visitors told me my friend was just now in surgery. Even though I wouldn't ever have wanted to see him again if he hadn't been hurt, I promised to call or visit the next day.

When I asked at the hospital, the information person had no record of my friend's being registered there. I eventually discovered that he'd been treated in the emergency room and released. As it turned out, while I'd tried to visit him in his hospital bed—when I thought he must be at death's door—he'd showed up for work. He'd looked like the walking dead and been able to see out of only one eye. He'd come in to repair people's bikes. My boss asked him not to come back. He never worked there again.

Since then I've been uncomfortable around him. I say hi, but I resist conversation. Tougher than me, he bounced right back and fixed his bike right away, even the wheels. Now, he and his bicycle look just like new.

Not me, though. I look different now, in my helmet. I think of it as a souvenir of that commute, a sort of memento mori, a reminder of my mortality. I hope my souvenir will shield me from sudden misfortune. My English friend had invited sudden Mr. Bad Luck into his life, but Bad Luck's a notorious party crasher. Bad Luck could call on any of us, uninvited.

I'm going to dress for the occasion.

DOUBLE-OH
THIRTEEN:
LICENSED TO RACE

HE STAYED there in a cabin in the Vermont woods, riding the fixed-gear bicycle into town once a week for groceries. He saw no one. He tried to forget.

Mornings, he'd sit in the sunlight that beamed through an opened window, eating whole-grain cereal with very little milk.

He kept himself fit because he knew no other way. No, not as fit as when everything was at stake, but fit, fit enough. Weights in the morning, it was, then a plain yogurt and half an apple before the 10-mile run in spiked 'cross shoes, carrying a rusty Varsity on his shoulder. Enough; that was enough.

His life was good, he thought, except when he'd climb off the wind trainer at 2:30 in the morning and just have to have sushi. Except for then; almost too good for too long.

The message surprised him, though it was delivered the usual way.

Messages were not coming, not supposed to come. He was past it now. He found this one inside what appeared to be a dandruff-shampoo sample.

Inside the sample box he found a Campy Super Record derailleur. Inside the derailleur, wrapped around the lower pivot bolt, inside the spring, he found an oiled paper. Written on that paper was a date, a time, and the initials of (so-called) Inspector 22.

"Here it is," he said to himself. "Here it is." And, sure enough, there it was.

His deeply hooded, grimly dark, but warmly sensitive eyes scanned the leafy Vermont distance. "The world," he thought, "is a small place indeed."

[Author's note: The world *is* small. Small, that is, until you're hungry and out of food on a lonely country road, your only spare already flat, and you've got 18 mountain miles to ride just to get to the first place you can buy a Hostess Fruit Pie. And it looks like rain. Then, the world is big.]

He sat at his perfect rolltop desk to set his affairs in order as he always did before these "trips." He reread his will— everything to Pedali Bodiddly Bicycle Club. He'd never met a member, but he liked the name.

He scanned his insurance policies and checked for mistakes on his USCF license. He found the word "united" misspelled twice but quickly forgave the federation its error. "It's their second language," he said to himself.

Satisfied now his papers were in order, he rose and entered his library. Leaning on a perfect antique chair was an old Frejus racing bicycle with a rod-operated front changer. When he deftly pivoted the changer lever seven millimeters toward the old bike's seat-tube, a wall of books slid noiselessly aside.

The vanished bookcase revealed a secret, flat-gray hidden wall, densely mounted with gleaming cycling gear. The hardware glistened against the dull-finished wood, glistened, lightly oiled, ready. "Ready," he thought, redundantly.

He looked at the wall and saw several complete bicycles: road

He kept himself fit because he knew no other way.

bicycles, track bicycles, and some that were said to go both ways. He saw wheels: disk wheels, spoked wheels, chainwheels, jockey wheels, and freewheels.

He saw special tools for every imaginable cycling need and some for needs for which, if you can imagine them, shame on you. He saw tools to fix things that, as of this writing, have never broken.

He saw conical stacks of freewheel cogs, bundles of butted spokes, six dozen stems, and seven spare saddles. He saw a gallon of Phil grease and two hatsful of headsets. He saw supplies enough to last the clumsiest novice racer through his first season. He surveyed the plethora of cycling paraphernalia and grunted. Good.

His hand, which could be cruel, gently brushed the top-tube of a

Gios. He snapped back the bike's rear derailleur, listening to the solid *thunk* as it sprung forward.

He spun a freewheel, listening to its smooth ratcheting whirr. He squeezed and released a brake lever: *click, click*. He spun a wheel, then tested its tire pressure with a flick of his fingernail: *ping, ping*. He slipped a wheel into the Gios fork and tightened the skewer: *noise of tightening skewer*.

He selected his favorite wrench, a Campy T-tool. It had been painstakingly smoothed, polished, and black-chromed by an aged Austrian bike mechanic whose identity had vanished from the world's computers. He looked at it; a perfect, realized T-wrench. He smiled.

He began to pack certain items from the wall into cases built by another old European craftsman, a Spaniard unknown to the Austrian or to anyone outside a select society, all of whom zealously guarded his identity and whereabouts. Always referred to by number, the Spanish artist's skills remained enveloped in mystery, even to his wife, who had no idea what he did all day.

The cases were designed, with infinite patience and cunning, to look like shoddy copies of inauthentic replicas of cheap designer luggage. Inside, though, ingeniously fitted high-density foam pro-tected each handcrafted glistening component. Cases full, he snapped each latch closed. He smiled again.

He thought of his assignment, the race. The race that meant so much to racing, to racing as we know it. He thought of faces he had not seen for years, faces of men who would give anything to know he was coming, but could not suspect.

He imagined the cold curve of the plastic-wrapped handlebar in his inhumanly strong but strangely graceful hands.

He smiled once again, a thin smile, almost cruel, and carried the cases out to the car.

A TOUGH CUSTOMER

HE WASN'T going to make any snap decisions, he said. He was shopping for a racing-type bicycle, under $1,500, preferably Italian. He'd been looking at a yellow Guerciotti at Shop B, our competition. They'd offered him an especially good deal.

"What do you have to show me," he asked, "that's kind of like that?"

I walked him by a couple of bikes, trying to get a handle on what he might like. I took him over to an Italian bike we had on sale, told him a little about it, and explained why I thought he might enjoy riding it.

He asked me a few dozen probing questions about bearings and bearing surfaces, spoke butting, clinchers versus sew-ups, saddle-rail metallurgy, silver and brass brazing, frame-tubing, fork offset, bottom-bracket height, and our store's warranty policy. My answers got shorter and shorter.

I pointed out that I thought we had the bike he was looking at in stock in his size. He said he hadn't quite decided what his size *was*. He hadn't talked to everyone yet (there was this guy in Nova Scotia), but he would know soon.

I felt relieved. I told him in technically precise terms that the bike in question, the bike he had his hand resting on right now, rode good. "You'll like it," I said.

"*Hmmm,*" he replied, "*hmmm.*"

He asked me if we would fit the bike to him if he decided to buy it. He liked the idea that he could get the stem or the toeclips changed especially for him. He asked about changing the stock gearing. I assured him that all would be made exactly as he wished.

"You'll like it," I said. "It handles good."

"*Hmmm,*" he replied, brows knitted, still unsure the seat-tube angle would place him in the proper position relative to the bottom bracket.

He said he would talk to me soon, thanked me for my 90 minutes, and left. He called twice in the next couple of days to clear up little problems, questions like: "Say, could you tell me if there's anything to all the talk about an Italian mystique?" Or, "Are you sure I don't need a mixed-tubing frame?"

Eventually he called and asked us to hold the bike until Saturday for him; he was for sure coming in to buy it. "Okay," I said, smiling prematurely.

Saturday came, and he did not come in. Weeks passed, and I forgot about him except when I'd notice that the nice bike he could have bought was still hanging in the shop instead of getting ridden, being useful.

Next time I saw him I was looking out the window of a gourmet coffee place, sipping an Aged Sulawesi and nibbling a moist bran muffin. I watched him walking his new yellow Guerciotti down the sidewalk as if he had it out for an airing. The bike looked so clean it was sinful to roll it down the tacky urban pavement.

It was painted a yellow so bright that if you leaned it on your bedroom wall and turned out the light, it'd still keep you up all night.

I smiled and waved, a high point of post-Athenian civilization. Mistaking my hearty greeting for a sincere one, he came right in to say hi.

I said, what a pretty bike, and he said, yeah he really liked it. He told me he'd gone into Store B many, many times while deciding to buy it. Maybe, in fact, 18 or 20 times, until the people who worked in Store B began to flinch when they saw him come in.

I felt stunned, unable to speak. I only stood there with my coffee waiting for what he'd say next.

He said he'd been out riding his new bike several times, and he'd been impressed by the response and the precise feel of the machine. I nodded, still unable to think of a thing to say. He said he'd been out on one long ride, and now his knees were hurting, bothering him.

Did I have any idea, he asked, what could be going on?

I asked him the same questions you'd have asked. Was he keeping his knees warm? He was. Was he staying in the low gears? He swore he was. Was his saddle adjusted right? He assured me he'd tried it up and down and fore and aft and tilted one way and the other. He felt it had to be perfect.

We discussed cleats and toeclip length and knee-over-bottom-bracket placement. We debated the merits of Fit-Kit cleat adjustment and considered whether the ball of one's foot should fall over, in front of, or behind a vertical line through the pedal axle.

Ever the good guy, the cycling enthusiast/salesman, I stood paralyzed there helping someone else's customer, answering one question after another. I was amazed at the guy's need for technical dialogue.

I asked him about the terrain he rode over. Was it hilly or mostly flat? A bit of both, he said. I asked him how low his lowest gear was. Did he use it? Was he climbing standing up or in the saddle? Did he feel he might be laboring at the pedals or rolling them around smoothly?

The gear was low enough, we decided. Yes, he used it and yes, he felt he was spinning the way he'd been told to do.

I looked at the brilliant yellow bike and at the sincere young man. As I looked, I could tell he was already forming his next question, like a pool hustler lining up the next shot.

I could feel myself getting old standing there, my hair graying, wrinkles spreading around my eyes. I asked him how far he'd ridden on the one long ride, the one that had caused all the havoc with his knees.

"Oh," he said, "about four miles, there and back."

"I see," I said, my throat suddenly dry.

"Well, you be careful out there," I told him, as I turned away toward the door. Not a moment too soon, I put the earnest young man and the canary bike and the good coffee smell farther and farther behind me.

THE BEST OF TIMES

I REMEMBER some of the best times at Bob's were the winters. In the winter months, training lost its urgency; our little group had time to hang around the shop and swap stories.

All of us tried to do some activity in the winter months to keep from gaining weight, but none of those substitutes took as much time as in-season road miles.

So afternoons found us watching the rain hit Bob's windows, building wheels or watching someone else build wheels, repacking hubs or headsets, and telling lies about what gear we'd been in at a certain time on a memorable ride.

These elaborate lies shared a predictable plot. The narrator would describe himself as a strict nonaggressor on such-and-such a no-pressure winter ride. He was just sitting in, he'd say, peaceably minding his own business. Some upstart, usually a younger guy, would throw down the gauntlet, offering some kind of subtle challenge. The frisky devil might be the narrator's best friend or his brother-in-law. Nonetheless, such wintertime nerviness demanded retribution.

I recall Bob Riley telling us this Big Ring tale one stormy Saturday at Bob's. Here's what he said:

"We went out on a flat ride, 12 or 14 of us, in what looked like a

'When I got out of the saddle to rocket past the guy, my right crank came off, then I came off in a manner most ungraceful.'

civilized group. Perfect winter ride. We sort of tempo'd out, rolling along pretty good, but smooth. Guys took short pulls. The sun was shining. I was wearing shorts for the first time in weeks. It was better'n perfect.

"When we hit those rollers out by the dam, some junior decided to dangle himself off the front up each climb. Every time, the guy behind him would have to bridge a little gap, and so would the guy behind that guy.

"So I said to the junior, 'We have such a nice smooth ride here. Can't you just go through at the front and get off?'

"He didn't say much. He eased off for about two turns and started in again.

"I was starting to get a little hot. These young guys, they think if they don't hammer on every ride, they're never gonna get a workout. Never fails; if you've got a bunch of guys working like a machine, one of those kids will attack and ruin it.

"Third time he came through too hard, I looked over and saw that Andy was shaking his head. The kid was getting to him, too. We were out there by the park. I was in maybe a 42×17, moving pretty good, but comfortable. The kid sat maybe 15 yards up the road.

"I looked behind; no traffic. I slipped out of line and jumped up behind him, still in my 17, and sat on his wheel.

"When he sensed me there, he picked up the pace ever so slightly. I never changed gear, just increased my speed to match. He saw I wasn't gonna just drop off his wheel. Instead of pulling over so I could come through, he sped up again, this time shifting up, obviously trying to ease me out of his draft.

"I saw him reach down to change gear; as he did, I slid as quietly as I could into my 15, so he wouldn't realize I'd shifted. You could see he was trying now; the fat was in the fire. His back began to sway, and he bent his arms more, leaning into the effort. I had to smile.

"We reached the top of the last hill. The junior looked back at me for just an instant, never easing the pace. I glanced back; the guys were well behind. It was just him and me.

"I saw him reach for the lever, and I saw his derailleur cage swing up and out. I resisted the temptation to use the big gear myself and spun the 42×15 as effortlessly as I could. I tried to control my breathing so he would think I was just coasting along behind him.

"We came around a corner and caught a tailwind. He grabbed a still higher gear and started inching away. I thought: 'Now is the time. This wind will make him feel like Fausto Coppi, but when I come around about 10 mph faster, he'll know the cruel truth.'

"I put it in the big ring.

"My bike was working great. I'd just done the complete overhaul on it, bottom bracket and everything. I felt sure I put the cranks on plenty tight enough. I got no warning, no creaking, nothing. When I got out of the saddle to rocket past the guy, my right crank came off, then I came off, in a manner most ungraceful.

"I think I fell for about half an hour. When everything stopped moving, I still had all my limbs, just like before, but I was bruised and scratched up. My shorts were torn so badly they barely hung on.

"The junior had stopped up the road, amazement all over his obnoxious junior face. The bunch rode up about then and, naturally, they asked me what had happened. I said my crank came off. No one had a tool to tighten it back on. When they satisfied themselves that I was okay, they rode away, wishing me good luck.

"I stood there with my crank in one hand, my bike in the other, trying to hold my shorts up with an elbow. I thought I'd stick my thumb out to try to hitch a ride home. It took me a few minutes to decide what to let go of. After a while I got a ride with a guy in an old van, me and my bike in the back with his sheepdog.

"I was off the bike a few days waiting for my road rash to stop weeping. Now my brake levers look more scratched up than they did. I don't mind a few scrapes and dents, all honorable wounds.

"The junior asked somebody where I lived and came over the next day to see how I was. He helped me retape my bars. He's kind of a nice kid.

"New riders like him, it's good if they have someone like me they can learn from."

FUN IN THE SUN

I WORKED in the caravan of the 1986 Coors Classic as a press motorcyclist, carrying Seth Goltzer, a photographer, on my Suzuki during the three road stages in California and Nevada.

I'd dreamed about riding in the caravan for eight months, since I heard I might have the opportunity. I had fantasies of the famous riders I would roll along beside and the fearsome descents I'd navigate at breakneck speed, meters in front of a gaining pack.

I invented scenarios of my masterful riding, elbow to elbow with The Badger (Bernard Hinault), The Hampster (Andy Hampsten), Steve Bauer, and Greg LeMond.

All my fantasies fell short of the reality. My little role in the Coors Classic was more fun than I imagined or could have imagined. And tenser than I could have conceived. It was four days in another galaxy. I brought back a few stories from that galaxy....

The race route for the Coors Classic in California is closed for the race by order of the state's governor. Closed. Both sides of the road. This closure guarantees a safe venue for the racers and a protected adult playground for the caravan. Imagine: scenic rural California highways sealed for our protection and pleasure, thank you. Savor that thought while I tell you what Seth and I did, exactly.

We followed either the break or the pack, in a group with the commissaire's car, the neutral support car, two press pickup trucks, numbers of team cars, other press motorcycles, and a few California Highway Patrol motorcycles.

Each caravan vehicle has a job to do, some jobs more urgent than others. Paul Koechli, the Red Zinger team director, felt lots of urgency when he'd speed up to talk to his riders in the breaks. He almost hit us three times.

Most of the race is over narrow two-lane roads. Usually Seth and I would ride in the left lane (closed, remember), which was reserved for press and for vehicles moving up and down the caravan. Koechli moved up and down aggressively, passing just when he wanted to, honking his horn, foot on the floor.

The Specialized-SunTour support car nearly took us out twice. It took both lanes to get that giant car around sharp downhill corners at speeds high enough to stay in front of the pack.

Seth and I would cruise behind the commissaire's car and wait for permission to pass through the pack or breakaway. When we got permission, we were to pass slowly and cautiously, clicking away, through the riders, who paid no attention at all. We had to plan which side to pass through on; they use both sides of the road, clear to the opposite edge on left-handers.

If we got caught in the peloton, we got a tongue-lashing from the commissaire. And the racers—yes, Bepe Saronni, Bernard, Phil Anderson, Greg, and all—would ride as close to us as if we were on a bicycle. So I was indeed banging elbows with my heroes, but I had to ride a 550-pound motorcycle with two men on it. Made me kinda nervous.

After we successfully passed through the racers we would rocket ahead several miles to some spot Seth would choose for a scenic shot. Many times we exceeded the speed limits by as much as, say, 30 mph. At each (closed) intersection, a CHP motor or patrol car officer would wave us by or give us a thumbs-up as we burned by. Euphoric.

CHP motor officers invariably rode in front of the race to check the security of the road. Those guys loved that duty. They'd ride side by side at 75 mph patrolling the curvy country roads. At one point, Seth and I followed two of them through bend after bend at 75 to 85 mph. It was surreal.

No matter how fast we went, a few minutes after we stopped, someone would be yelling, "Here they come!" The race covers ground at a terrific rate. On one Sierra climb, a long, long grind, Seth and I maintained a steady gap in front of an eight-man break. My speedometer needle sat on 22 mph. Inside my helmet I shook my head in disbelief. The stages were *so* long, the climbs *so* hard....

The level of bike handling skill was awesome. The cornering speeds at the criteriums were impossible, I thought, but I always think that. The racers looked as if they were born on their bikes. I watched at the feed zones. A rider would grab a musette, sling it over his shoulder, take the food packets and bottles out, and stow them in jersey pockets and cages, all without slowing or wavering at all.

Seth and I stopped at a beautiful bridge at the bottom of the long, winding descent just out of Nevada City. Somehow, Hinault, Anderson, and six others had gained over a minute on that descent, against the finest bike riders in the world. *How is that done?* I wondered.

We rode next to Steve Bauer on the Squaw Valley–to–Reno stage. Solo, he chased down a two-man break. The feat took miles of effort. He rode calmly and apparently unhurriedly, closing the gap meter by meter.

Seth, all excited, yelled at him once, "Go, Steve," but Bauer never looked up. His attention stayed on his work. More excitement shot through the crowd and the caravan when he made contact, then slowed the break so his teammate LeMond could win the field sprint in Reno. Bauer just did his job, did what his team manager directed. The heroism is in *our* eyes—the eyes of the press and fans.

I saw and talked with *my* heroes at the Coors Classic. Bepe Saronni appears to speak no English and to be a little preoccupied. Raul Alcala looks great on his bike. I walked by him and said, "Buena suerte, Raul," and he beamed as if he'd won the lottery.

Davis Phinney was as approachable and chatty as ever. Bob Roll said the mountain stages were, "not so bad if you were feeling good, really hard if you weren't." Todd Gogulski of the U.S. national amateur team was super, waxing philosophical after the races. Jonathan Boyer was as cordial and personable as he always is.

A real thrill for me was meeting and talking with Dietrich "Didi" Thurau, of West Germany. Perhaps you remember Didi from his early days with Peter Post's Raleigh team in Europe. Thurau was the young sensation then. He was always beautiful on a bike, poetry. He still is. He's tall and big for a racer, has curly blond hair and movie-star good looks. He turned out to speak excellent English.

When I rode the motorcycle up to him he was standing by his bike, looking at the mountains around Squaw Valley, not a bad way to pass the time. I told him he was a hero of mine, that I had thought we'd never meet, and how pleased I was.

He thanked me and asked me if I also rode a bicycle and if I raced. He asked me if I enjoyed the Coors Classic. He stood there in the Squaw Valley sunshine, surrounded by mountains, and smiled.

"It's so beautiful here," he said.

"Yes, Didi," I said. "I think so too."

IN ONE ERA;
OUT THE OTHER

AT THE Reno bicycle trade show, if you stood in just the right spot, you could see into two eras. From right in front of the little Hetchins booth, you could see both the one Hetchins frame and the big splashy Screamin' Eagle frame booth across the way.

You did not have to elbow through a crowd of *oohers* and *aahers* to admire the Hetchins. Across the aisle, on the other hand, the Screamin' Eagle booth was jammed with people talking business. High-tech Screamin' Eagle business is good; Hetchins-style business, I believe, is quieter.

Hetchins bicycles could only be English. They are emblems of a prouder British past, when that nation was an industrial giant, and craftsmanship was in flower. A Hetchins frame represents hours of painstaking hand construction by the builder himself. The man whose name is on the frame built it. That's an old-fashioned–sounding idea today, isn't it?

The Hetchins frame model that's become most famous (known to several dozen people in the U.S.) is the "curly-stay," characterized by gracefully bowed seatstays and chainstays. In 1988, those curved frame tubes look antique and quaint, but still lovely.

Hetchins frames have curved tubes because back a few decades ago, the rules governing bicycle racing in England prohibited framemaker decals. Officials thought that advertising on the bikes tainted the pure amateur sport. But builders wanted readers of *Cycling,* the weekly paper, to be able to spot their products in race photos. They developed personal frame designs fans could identify without decals. They used such curiosities as curly rear triangles, funny-shaped forks, and seat stays that joined the top tube inches in front of the seat cluster. Charming stuff.

Hetchins frames are available in several grades, varying in the fantastic detail work. Most Hetchins that reach the U.S. feature incredibly ornate hand-cut lugs and fork crowns. The filigreed fork-crown trim often extends a couple of inches down the fork blades. The bottom-bracket tangs and brake-bridge trim could be equally fancy. Someone very skilled spends hours and hours fashioning those lugs and crowns, probably someone named Hetchins. The frameset I saw at the Reno show had it all. Gee, it was beautiful.

Across the aisle, surrounded by nice '80s folks, was the new-as-tomorrow Screamin' Eagle, computer-designed, made of something or other from aerospace research, and looking ever so sleek and state-of-the-art. I didn't ask anybody, because I was in no position to act on the answer, but I'll bet the price of the Hetchins and the Screamin' Eagle are close to the same.

I'll also bet that curvaceous new Screamin' Eagle is great to ride. I'm willing to believe claims that it flexes not at all in the vicinity of the bottom bracket. I'll concede that it has chainstays that could strike awe into the hearts of bridge abutments in the matter of rigidity.

I'll even admit that the one-piece look might grow on an owner, that he or she might, in time, get to like it. I'll even go along with test reports that the pricey device combines track-bike stiffness with boulevard ride. I still don't want one.

But perhaps you do. And perhaps you're in a position to afford one. There are lots of reasons to buy a bike like a Screamin' Eagle, and there'll be lots of encouraging, admiring voices. Here's a tiny note of dissension from a guy who would never claim to be objective. My argument is entirely emotional. There's nothing the matter with those bikes.

But when you buy a Hetchins, or a Serotta, or a DeRosa, or a U.S. Terry, you are paying for hand assembly of known components. You are paying for a certain number of hours spent by an artisan who, in many cases, has *you* in mind. The frames cost good money because tubesets and lugs and hours of a craftsperson's time cost good money.

Perhaps the first Screamin' Eagle, or the first thousand Screamin' Eagles, will be expensive to produce. Soon, however, the economies of scale and the reduced need for skilled hand labor will bring the cost down, first to the builder, then to the eventual customer. High-tech will become everyday. There will be Screamin' Eagle clones available at hardware stores.

Let's say you buy one of the new Screamin' Eagles, let's call it Model One. A component of your desire for that frame will be its stature as the Latest Thing. Sadly, a year from now or a month from now, those rascally Screamin' Eagle constructors will unveil Model Two, and perhaps Three, the deluxe version with all the glue-ons. Your bike will ride just as well, but it will have lost its "ultimacy." Has to happen. Part of what you paid for has vanished.

Every Hetchins ever sold remains a source of pride to its owner. So does every DeRosa, every Serotta. Truly handmade bikes will never flood the market, because craftspersons' hands can only work so fast. And a year-old Eisentraut loses nothing, in real or perceived value.

Because bicycles are so perfected, because they do not have motors, because they can only do what you are able to cause them to do, there are only tiny differences between the dozens of good ones. By opting for the latest, trickest thing, you set yourself up for eventual dissatisfaction. It's never the latest for long.

And the truth is: if you and your buddy go to the races, you on your new-as-now monument to far-seeing science and your friend on his stone-age, brazed-up, butted-steel sled, whichever of you is stronger and smarter will prevail. That's a wonderful aspect of cycling, and it's an aspect some people would prefer you forgot. Long enough for your credit card approval to light up the screen.

NAMEDROPPERS

"GOOD EVENING, ladies and gentlemen. Welcome to *Namedroppers*, the prime (pronounced preem)-time cycling quiz show with total racing FAN-tasy Fulfillment Potential.

"Here's how our show works: each contestant answers a series of increasingly demanding questions about bicycle racing history. Twenty-eight correct answers qualify the contestant for a chance at FAN-tasy Fulfillment. He or she is asked 12 additional truly difficult questions from the annals of cycling competition.

"Twelve correct answers, and here is what happens: the lucky and knowledgeable prize winner—let's say it's you—gets to choose a star from the current racing champions.

"For example, you may think that Davis Phinney has a pretty fair finish, that he might be hard to beat in a last-200-meters situation. You have, let's say, always yearned for the ability to pulverize Phinney in a sprint, to stomp him into tearful submission in front of his hometown crowd, say, or at a classic, watched by millions.

"So you choose Phinney. You also choose another star, one of your all-time favorites, for the FAN-tasy confrontation. Let's say you choose handsome '60s and '70s Bianchi pro Felice Gimondi, whose star shone brightly even during the decade-long heyday of Eddy Merckx.

"The expert *Namedroppers* staff outfits you in perfect period clothing, in this case the sky blue and white wool of the Bianchi squad. The staff fits you to a late-'60s Bianchi racing bicycle, green with blue trim, white cotton tape, Universal sidepulls—just like in the pictures.

"You and your bicycle are flown to Roubaix, France, along with Phinney and his 7-Eleven support personnel. You meet the *Namedroppers* crew there, already set up for a meticulously staged duplication of the last segment of the Paris-Roubaix classic.

"Filming begins about 30 kilometers from Roubaix. Staffers liberally coat you and Phinney with mud. Then you're off on the bikes. Cameras watch as you eye each other warily in a rapidly dwindling pack. The brutal pace has taken its toll on the less fit, the mere supermen, leaving only a few godlike athletes still on their bikes.

"There is you, as Gimondi. There are Phinney and five or six others. You all look bad.

"Occasionally, team cars drive up, and men hand you bottles. The *Namedroppers* cameraman in your car focuses on your dull, glazed eyes, framed by the spattered mud that is coating most of your face. You look fried, but your pedal stroke is regal, perfect.

"Helicopters overhead film the slow attrition as rider after rider drops away. Soon, it's just you and Phinney, relaying each other. The outskirts of Roubaix come into sight. Each of you does his share, stretching the gap between you and the exhausted stragglers.

"There'll be no surprises now. It'll be Gimondi (*you!*) or Phinney. Tension resonates in the air. Mobs of fans divide just in time for the two of you to pass through.

"The velodrome appears. You and Phinney, out of your saddles, ride through the tunnel to the track. Your first visual image, as the roar of the crowd slams your ears, is the somehow familiar five girls in four-inch skirts dancing in the infield.

"That's right. They're your own high school cheerleaders, from your junior year, girls who looked right through you in the halls. It's true. They're here, screaming in hot-blooded frenzy, for *YOU*, compliments of *Namedroppers*.

"The track announcer screams into his mike. The crowd degenerates from unruly to berserk. Phinney chooses his moment and jumps, confident of his speed. You dig down for it all and grab his wheel. Sensing you there, he eases off. Just a lap and a half to go.

"You ride up alongside. Phinney's face looks white under the mud. You jump as hard as you've ever done anything in your life. Damn, he's on your wheel, on it like paint. Nothing to do but ride it out now, ride like you were chased by the hangman. One lap, a few hundred meters. Less now as Phinney starts to come around.

"It's wheel to wheel, but he falters. Phinney falters. Just for a heartbeat Davis Phinney falters, and it's you. It's you—at the line it's *YOU*, and the cameras are rolling, and the fans are rioting, and the helicopters beat the air, and the announcer is drooling into his microphone.

"You roll down a lap and stop. Someone gently wipes the mud off your face and puts a clean Bianchi hat, brim up, on your head. Someone else puts a huge, extravagant victory wreath around your neck and kisses you. It's your Senior Prom Queen, flown from her job at the Montessori School in Teaneck, New Jersey, to be here for you, today.

"'Way to go, animal,' she says.

"Wearing the wreath, you do a hands-in-the-air promenade lap of the velodrome, basking in the crowd's adulation. At home, you would crash and humiliate yourself trying to ride that far no-hands, but today you rise to the occasion.

"On the victory stand, cameras study your face as you watch the no-hopers come in, barely pedaling, helpless victims of the pace set by you and the now crestfallen Phinney.

"Other cameras watch as you put a consoling arm around him. 'There'll be another day, Davis,' you seem to be saying.

"A few days after your return home, *Namedroppers* will ship a giant-screen TV and VCR to your bicycle club so the professionally produced and edited video story of your victory can be shown at meetings. You are provided with copies of the tape so you can enjoy home viewing and use them for delightful personalized gifts.

"You become a member of the *Namedroppers* Winners Club. You will receive a copy of each subsequent winner's tape so you can watch

Welcome to Namedroppers, the prime-time cycling quiz show.

as a current champion is brutally crushed by someone much like yourself.

"If you'd like to be a guest on our show, please send a recent photo, a copy of your yellowed last expired racing license and, in 25 words or less, explain why you've always wanted, on Peewee Herman's bicycle, to ride away from Andy Hampsten on L'Alpe d'Huez.

"Send the above to Rusty Fixed-Cupp, 5313 Lois Lane, Kilo, Colorado 10885."

REACH OUT
AND TOUCH SOMEONE

THURSDAYS I try to go long. I've usually raced on Sunday. If I ride long earlier in the week I've probably not had time to recover from Sunday. There's always Friday and Saturday to take it easy and get fresh for the next race.

Not everyone I ride with does things that way. So there I was last Thursday, all by myself in the middle of a four-and-a-half-hour training ride, when I saw another cyclist up ahead.

Sure enough, as I got closer I could see it was a woman, moving right along and looking pretty good on the bike. As I rode up alongside her, I moved over to the center line so as not to surprise her and said hi.

"Hi," she said. "What a great day for a ride."

"Really," was about the wittiest thing I could think of to say. I asked her where she'd started her ride. She'd come from the suburban town next to mine. That meant that she was on a substantial bike ride.

We rode along together for 5 or 10 miles. She had no trouble on the little rolling hills, and she seemed to handle her bike just fine. She wore what I call tourist-style clothing, a fairly plain wool jersey and dark blue cotton shorts with bulging side pockets.

She must have assumed I was a racer. We didn't talk about bike racing, but my club jersey and shaved legs surely gave me away. After a few miles, she asked me why serious cyclists act so unfriendly.

Lots of times, she said, other riders wouldn't wave or respond to a greeting. She told me that sometimes guys coming up behind her would sprint by; they wouldn't speak or nod, or even acknowledge her presence in the road.

She'd been a runner, she said, and almost all the runners had smiled and waved at each other. Why weren't cyclists like that?

"Hey," I said, taking it personally, "did I just roll by?"

"No, you're real nice. But, you know, you're the first person who looks like a serious rider I've talked to, outside a bike shop," she said.

I couldn't understand. Here was this attractive young lady, pleasant, easy to talk to, getting ignored and snubbed on the road by other cyclists. At the same time, I could remember passing plenty of riders myself who just stared straight ahead as if in a trance and couldn't be bothered to say hi.

"It's not just you," I said. "It happens to me. I'll see other bikies who are evidently committed riders, maybe loaded tourists or racers in sponsors' jerseys. The same thing will happen. It's strange."

"Are all you guys so deadly serious about riding? Is every training ride so important?" she asked. "I know some pretty competitive runners who always have time to wave."

The woman and I eventually took different routes back to our homes, but I couldn't stop thinking about our conversation. What kind of guy knocks himself out to pass a woman rider, just so he can feel stronger than she?

Some of those guys, who rode right by without speaking, are telling their buddies this minute that they'd like to meet nice women who rode bicycles and understood a little about the sport. I met that woman 30 miles out into the countryside. Any person who has pedaled that far alone on a ride and has at least as far to pedal to get home understands the sport.

I thought about how relatively few people we meet who are

somewhat like ourselves: who take care of themselves, think about diet and rest, and actually ride their bikes.

So why the snobbery? Clearly, there are subgroups within cycling, each secretly imagining itself to possess a certain elite status.

There is the solitary, self-sufficient tourist. There is the resolute, rain-or-shine commuter, the Italophile racer, the hard-training triathlete, the muddy-booted mountain biker. It seemed to me, though, that they all turn the pedals in a circle; they have more in common than they like to admit.

Each one of them is attempting to do more than just sit home with his or her feet up watching Richard Simmons, drinking diet cola, and sincerely intending to smoke less.

It occurred to me that if motorcyclists, who cannot recognize each other behind their helmets, and owners of the same brand of automobile, who may have nothing else in common, can wave at each other, we can too.

So—say hi to another cyclist today. Do it for me, as a favor. I admit that practice will not prevent flat tires, nor will it shield you from our friends in baseball caps driving pickup trucks. But you and I will know, and we'll appreciate it, and so will the woman I rode with.

And really, *really*, what harm can it do?

CARLOS

"WE'RE THINKING about starting a team," Carlos said, "kind of a development team, just for Cat IIIs. There'd have to be a few decisions made, like who'd be on the team, who'd get jerseys, and who'd get travel money. We'd need a little managing. Your name was mentioned."

"Jeez, that's flattering," Russell said. "But I don't think I'm exactly the man you want. I have had a little experience running a team, but you know, I think I'm a little pessimistic."

Carlos told him that it wouldn't be a lot of work running the team, really it wouldn't. A guy would just choose who got skinsuits, maybe plan a little race strategy, that's all. Easy.

"I ran that team, Carlos," Russell said after a minute, "all experienced guys, guys who'd been to lots of races, all over. Mostly they knew the others from seeing them around. They liked each other.

"They were excited, I think, about getting on that team, getting a little help with their racing. They liked getting a bike, some clothes, their registrations paid, transportation paid.

"They said they were excited about participating in a *team*. Beyond a certain point, bike racing's a team sport, as I'm sure you know, but a team's a difficult thing, hard to create. I did my best," Russell said, "and I confess I was disappointed with the results. Not the race results, the personal results."

"What happened?" Carlos asked.

"Well," Russell said slowly, "the guys had a certain amount of difficulty getting along together. Even guys who'd been friends, guys who used to call each other between races, got to hate each other. Called each other names.

"'So-and-so wouldn't block for me when I got in the break.' Or, 'So-and-so chased me down when I was away, brought 15 guys up to the break I was in.' That's how they'd talk. Got kinda discouraging."

"Why didn't guys help each other?" Carlos asked.

"Self-interest," Russell said deliberately. "Guys with the best intentions, guys who say they have the strongest desire to ride in a *team* situation, will, in the heat of racing, do what's best for themselves. I don't like the sound of that when I say it, but I'm afraid it's the sad truth."

Carlos said he thought the guys in his club would help each other.

"Maybe they would," Russell said. "On pro teams, a guy gets paid to do a job in races. He's not paid to win, necessarily, or to take one prime sprint after another. He's paid to do his best to get his team's strongman in position to finish well. Sometimes he gets paid *not* to finish. Amateur racers only have results and prizes to ride for.

"This team I ran," Russell went on, "guys could get more than just prizes. You could get airplane tickets to far-away places. You could get hotel money and food money and tires. We had a team car.

"There were good reasons to ride for the team. Even so, guys would sit at the back and watch a teammate ride away in a small break. They'd sit at the back and sprint for 10th place instead of going right to the front to shut down the field for their teammate.

"They'd have all kinds of elaborate excuses why they didn't block, or even worse, why they towed the pack up to the break. They'd say they figured the other guys in the break could outsprint their teammate, or the teammate might get dropped on some hill up the road. Always some excuse. And it was hard for me to know what was right, since I was never with them there in the pack.

"But here's what I'm driving at, Carlos," Russell said. "If we couldn't motivate guys to ride as a team, with all the stuff we had to offer, how're you gonna motivate Cat IIIs?"

"Let's say you're the second-best criterium rider on the team. Are you going to ride race after race taking care of your teammate, making sure he doesn't have to chase down a break by himself? Are you going to lead him out early and hard and never contest the sprint yourself?"

"I think I'd be the best Cat III criterium rider in the club," Carlos said.

"Oh, I see," Russell laughed. "Well, then, I suppose you'll have guys sacrificing their results so you can upgrade by June. But, think about it. What's in it for them? Are you going to split your prizes? How will you split a cheap sew-up tire?"

Carlos said he thought he was starting to see what Russell was talking about.

"I think we're still going to try," Carlos said. "Yours wasn't the only name mentioned. Some people thought I might make a pretty good manager myself."

"Hey, I think you might make a really good manager," Russell said. "Everyone likes you and respects you. Now I'm feeling kind of bad; I painted such a gloomy picture. There were times when it was great.

"I had this one guy on the team I didn't know hardly at all when the season started, a young guy. He never asked for anything, and if you gave him a new chainring bolt he got excited. He got excited about stuff: you could say, hey, we're gonna do this, or we're gonna do that, whatever. He'd say, *I'm stoked*. What a kid.

"Anyway," Russell went on, "we went down to southern California for this two-day race, a road race Saturday, a criterium on Sunday. This kid I'm talking about had won the road race the previous year, wanted to win again if he could. Well, he blew up. It was hot as hell, huge hill every lap. He blew up.

"I remember him sitting next to the road on the ground, apologizing to me that he hadn't done better. I think he was almost crying. He wanted to show his new team manager how much he could offer his team.

"Sunday at the criterium we had one rider after another drop out. The guys who'd done well at the road race were tired. They rode a while and quit. We had a flat tire or two, and there was no free lap. Bad luck. One guy's freewheel blew up. We went down there with maybe 10 guys; suddenly we had three left in a pack of 75 or 80.

"Last lap you could see them coming around a bend on the far side of the course. This little group of us was standing in the pit area watching. You could see that one guy had a little distance, serious distance, really, on the last lap, on all those guys. It was hard to tell how fast the pack was moving, that close to the finish, but you can bet it was fast.

"The guy standing next to me says, 'By God, that looks like one of our jerseys.' Well, by God, it *was* one of our jerseys: it was the kid, who'd blown up the day before. He was putting it on the best field southern Cal had to offer, in the most dramatic possible way—in a last-lap, perfectly timed, solo move. I was transported.

"I've got a picture," Russell said, "of my girlfriend trying to hug me from behind while I'm jumping up and down in joy from that kid's winning the race.

"Hey, Carlos, I'm saying now that it's not all as bad as I was telling you before. Well, some of it's that bad, but not all. That's what I think now that I've had a minute, now that I've had a chance to think about it a little more."

JILL

MOST OF the time, she'll say, "No, you go ahead and ride with the guys. I'll just hold you up."

And I say, "No you won't. C'mon and ride with us. I rode hard yesterday. I don't need a workout today."

So she says, "Okay, if you're sure I won't hold you back."

And I say, "No. I like to ride with you, and we don't get the chance to get out together nearly often enough."

So we get on our bikes, and we come down here to Bob's to meet the guys. The ride starts off slow, all right, with everybody warming up, but pretty soon some glandular type like Tony or Jack gets frisky, and the hammer goes down.

I ride along with Jill and watch the guys fade into the distance. I feel a little bit bad, 'cause I would have enjoyed riding with them, but not too bad, 'cause I really do like to cruise along with Jill and talk and all.

Then *she* feels bad. She's sure I'm covering up my disappointment at not being with the bunch. Nothing I say makes any difference. I would be having a good time, but she's so sure I'm miserable because of her, she gets grumpy. That ruins what could have been a pleasant ride in the country.

I don't know what to do. If I don't ride with her, she worries that we don't do things together like we used to. If I do, she thinks I'm loafing and bored.

Hey, it's not like she can't ride well. Sometimes she goes really good—I mean, when it's her idea. She has to believe she's suffering because she enjoys it, not just to keep up with me or my friends.

Last year on the Two Rock ride, Jill couldn't be dropped. We had that great paceline going, remember, 8 or 10 of us? There was no way to get her off a wheel. And she loved it, going fast with the boys.

If we had more flat country around here, she'd never get dropped. You know that ride the Wheelmen have every year up around the lake in Solano County? I took her with me two years ago. I had to kinda get her up for it. Big ride like that with lots of well-known racers—I guess she was a little intimidated.

Anyway, I'd been off my bike a week or so myself. First I had a cold, then I got busy at work. The days had started getting shorter, and I hadn't had time to train. Still, I was excited about the ride.

Well, it started off really fast. George was there, and Cully, and what's-his-name from Hayward. Probably those guys didn't think it was so fast, but I was impressed, and immediately in trouble. The strain of the fast start hit my legs hard. All I could do was hang on to the back of the group. I wouldn't have dared take a pull. One pull would have done me in.

Meanwhile, Jill rode like a pro. She went to the front two or three times and took short pulls, saving her energy. A couple of times, she flashed me great smiles.

Me, I could not smile. I could only hurt. I thought about my recent cold, about the long hours I spend standing on my feet at work, about the weeks of nontraining. I hung grimly on at the back of the line, but my miles were numbered.

When the hill came, I came off. I don't remember the pace being so hard on that hill; it wasn't brutal, but I got sawed right off. I had almost 30 more cold, windy miles to ride, back to the car and the post-ride lunch. As miserable as I got, I never thought of turning back. I did think, though, of my old, good friend, the small chainring, but even it was cold comfort in the headwind.

Jill had disappeared over the hill with the pack. I was as happy for her as a person in my sorry state could have been, I guess. I sat there on my Italian superbike, dumbly pedaling off the miles, no style or class, feeling worse and worse.

How long, I wondered, can it take to ride 28 miles? Time trialists do almost that distance in 54 minutes. I thought about all the training miles in my legs. Surely they would remember all those miles, surely they would bounce back. They did not remember. They did not bounce back.

Halfway between the hill and the end of the ride, I began to feel a little hungry, and weaker, and even more miserable.

Then I had a flat.... No, I didn't really have a flat, but that's what you were expecting, weren't you? You thought I would tell you about my flat, how I pried the punctured tubular off the rim with frozen fingers. Then maybe my spare would turn out to be no good. Real Jack London stuff. But that's not what happened.

I finished the ride, is what happened. Any bikie who has ever bonked or finished a long ride alone and disappointed can imagine how I felt when I saw the town, the cars, and the restaurant.

All the bikes had been packed into and onto cars when I arrived. I pictured my friends sitting at long tables with checkered tablecloths, eating huge chunks of French bread out of baskets, sipping red wine and wondering which of the delicious dinners to order.

I left my bike on the restaurant porch. I leaned that bike, my pride and joy, against the wall with the same regard drivers feel for the one old sneaker they see abandoned in the road.

I steadied myself and entered, comforting my shattered self-esteem with the thought that maybe some of the guys figured I had actually flatted.

The smell of all that food hit me and made me light-headed. I spied the long table where Jill and my pals were sitting. I noted she had saved a place for me. I sat down and grabbed a chunk of bread with one hand and the butter dish with the other.

Jill smiled at me the way she does. "Gee," she said, "what a great ride."

THE HARD SELL

"HELLO," THE fellow said, "I want to buy a bicycle."

"Right," I said. "What kind of bicycle did you have in mind?"

"Well, I'd like something made of good tubing, preferably double butted," he answered.

I told him that even to be shown such a thing would require a note from his mother. I make remarks like that one to put people at their ease and give them a glimpse of my cleverness. This fellow, who was about 30, just looked at me.

"Good tubing and a lugged frame are what I'm thinking about," he said.

He pronounced lugged "lug-ged," as in rugged. We walked a few steps to a medium-priced sport bike that we sell in quantity, a favorite of most of the employees here. The fellow stood back from it and shook his head.

"What color is that?" he asked.

"Gray," I answered. "Charcoal gray."

"I really don't like that color," he said. "How much does this bike weigh?"

I told him the bike weighed 24 pounds, which it did. He said he wanted something lighter, maybe around 21 or 22 pounds, including a luggage rack, seat bag, and two bottles.

I watched him put his hands on the saddle once, then twice. 'Buy this bike,' I said.

"Ah," I answered, "I'm beginning to get a clearer picture of what you're thinking about. Step over here."

I showed him a super-clean, almost unridden built-up touring bike we had on consignment, a no-expense-spared, top-flight, nice bike. I like this bicycle, even though I need a touring bike like a crocodile needs *The Christian Science Monitor*.

"This is nice," he said, "but awfully heavy." He wanted raised sit-up handlebars, he went on, shaking his finger at the Cinelli Model 64s, and he wondered if it would be possible to put the gear levers in the ends of those bars. Oh, and did we have these in any other colors?

I felt like a sporting goods salesman must feel when the customer to whom he's showing the top-grade, engraved shotgun reveals he intends someday to bag his limit in beer bottles off his back fence.

Unruffled, light-footed, I adeptly changed course in mid-speech.

"Take a look at this," I suggested, pointing out one of the new fat-tire urban cruisers. "This bike has touring-style bars for comfortable upright seating and good visibility. It has handy thumb-operated gear levers on the bars and mountain-bike-style brakes for secure all-weather stops." I speak fluent Brochure.

"This machine has sealed bearings, sealed beams, and beamed

ceilings. It has investment-cast, high-pressure, flat semisloping, quick-release, forged bottle-cage tubing decals. You'll find it requires very little maintenance," I said, stressing convenience. Today's fat-tire cruiser is so often a busy man.

"This is getting a little closer," he said. "A little more like it. The tires, though, aren't they sort of, well, fat?"

"Fat. Yes, they are fat, and proud of it," I said. I told him about northern California, about how a few young American men had taken a few old American bicycles and created a wheeled art form that would keep several Taiwanese factories on double shifts for years.

I saw his head lift, his eyes brighten with pride.

I told him about the early days, the pioneers. I told him about modified beach bikes, about derailleur conversions, about one-piece cranks. I described fearless men and sheer descents. I asked him to buy that bike, there and then.

"Phew," he said, "you really have been helpful. But I've only just started looking. This is the first place I've stopped. What other makes of bikes would you suggest I investigate?"

I considered suggesting he investigate public transportation. I thought about changing jobs. I thought about paying retail for silk sew-ups. I felt new resolve.

I walked him into Little Italy, the corner of the store wherein we have enshrined the one full-blown professional superbike we can afford to stock. This one was a team-replica Glandulo, chromed and engraved and decaled within a millimeter of parody.

"Nice, huh?" I expounded.

"Wow!" he said.

I told him about Coppi, about Gimondi, about *pavé* and *tifosi*. I explained time trials and echelons and complex carbohydrates. I told him about the hour record and my method for keeping a chamois soft.

I watched him put his hand on the saddle once, then twice. "Buy this bike," I said.

"My luggage rack.... My flat bars...."

"Isn't done," I said gently.

"Credit cards," he asked, his mouth dry. "Do you take credit cards?"

"Reluctantly," I answered, as my fingers closed around the plastic.

A MAN AND HIS DOG

IF I'D known then that he would hit me barely a half-hour later, I'd have paid more attention when I first saw him. I do remember that the scene where I first saw him struck me as so bizarre I remarked on the strangeness of it to the woman I was riding with.

We'd ridden almost 60 miles of a fine-weather spring century, she and I, pedaling along together almost from the start. We'd chat awhile and hammer awhile, well matched in both activities.

I led as we dropped down steeply into a tiny Sierra foothill town. We had to slow for traffic in a village so small its city limit signs were nearly back to back. A dog had been hit and killed just seconds before we got there. As we pedaled by, I could see that dog lying in the road, a thin stream of blood from its mouth bright on the blacktop.

I saw the man who would hit me standing over the dog, straddling the white line dividing the lanes, glaring at the oncoming cars and glaring at *us*. Something about his stare chilled me.

That man has a vigilante look, I thought. A look that said he knew lots of things in the world were flat wrong; when he could, by God, he'd put them right. The dog's violent death was part of the chaos that man could sense on our streets and highways.

It struck me that we probably were parts of the chaos too, the woman and I, a couple of pain-in-the-ass bicyclers like the dozens strung out up and down his local road. He'd show us.

Sunny, rolling miles passed. The woman and I passed a fellow on a Bob Jackson touring bike for the third time that day, the way fast riders will if they like to stop and eat M&M's at the rest points.

As we passed the Jackson, she led. I remember us rolling along at a pretty fair pace, with me just behind and diagonally to her left, right on the white line at the edge of the road.

The left side of my vision turned dirty orange, and something loud whacked my arm, bouncing me and my bike over about a foot and a half. My front wheel just missed her back wheel. I held on and managed to stay upright. I got my bike stopped and climbed off. The rust-colored van that had hit me pulled over onto the road shoulder just ahead and stopped.

My friend gaped. "What happened?" she said.

I told her I'd been hit but I was okay. I checked my elbow. It was bleeding but not badly hurt. My hip ached. I decided he'd got my elbow with his mirror and my hip with the side of the van. I got that oh-man-that-was-close feeling.

It occurred to me the van looked familiar. I realized I'd seen it before, several times before, along the century route. I concluded it must be a support or sag vehicle. I thought, "I've been hit by a member of the club that's putting on this ride."

Right away I felt sorry for the guy. "He'll be mortified," I thought.

The Jackson rider jumped off his bike, all excited. He'd seen it all, he said, everything. The van had swerved into me, he said, not me into the van.

I watched the driver get out of his van and stride toward me. It didn't dawn on me at first that he was the same guy I'd seen standing in the road.

He looked at me and asked me just exactly what was going on here. I asked him if he were part of the ride, working on the century. "Huh?" he said.

He didn't know what the *hell* I was talking about, he said, but if I had a *problem* we could talk about it right here.

Just then, like a God from a machine, a sheriff's car drove up, and at that instant I realized that this was the man from the surreal dying-dog scene. As the sheriff got us organized to tell him what we'd seen, one by one, my normally mellow friend Tony rode up, braked abruptly to a stop, dropped his megabuck showbike to the ground, and screamed at the van driver.

"You son of a bitch," he shrieked, "you've been following this ride trying to scare cyclists. Now you've hit my friend. I'm gonna take your goddam head off!"

Tony looked at the deputy standing there calmly taking it all in. He told the deputy that the van driver had skimmed as close to single riders and groups as he could, scaring Tony and his wife in the process. The two of them had watched him drive crookedly up the road, watched that van barely miss one rider after another. Tony, trust me, was hot.

First the deputy took me aside, and we talked. Then he talked to the van driver, then the witnesses. He told us that if the incident was, in fact, accidental, the Highway Patrol would handle the proceedings. If the police thought the action was deliberate, his own county department would take charge. He went to his patrol car to radio for CHP assistance.

My woman friend and I walked Tony up the road a ways to calm him down. Me, I'd never got upset. I looked at the van driver, trying to understand. What kind of man, I wondered, threatens what may have been dozens of cyclists with his truck, then hits one, parks, and asks his victim what the hell *his* problem is?

I'd say the guy probably stood about five-seven. He was clean cut, and he held himself in what I'd call a military way. His chin stuck out like a Marine drill instructor's. He had every muscle tensed tight.

While we waited for the Highway Patrol, he took a dog out of his van and walked it on a leash up and back on the shoulder. As he went by, I couldn't resist scratching the dog behind the ears. Hey, it seemed like a nice enough dog, and it probably wasn't driving when he hit me. I felt we had plenty of evidence against the driver. The law would take care of him. No need for me to feel angry.

Two very sympathetic CHP officers arrived and took statements from all the concerned parties. I never could hear what the van driver said about the accident. Mostly, he stood spread-legged at the edge of the road, silent, arms folded, chin out.

After the interdepartmental discussion, the policemen told us they thought the collision had been deliberate. The Nevada County Sheriff's Department would proceed. We got back on our bikes to finish our ride. I noted, surprised, that the assembled officers permitted my assailant to drive off as if nothing had happened.

Once on the bike, I made extra sure I rode well over on the shoulder. I noticed I was a little jumpy when I heard cars approaching from behind. These getting-hit kinds of experiences can have you looking back behind you, take it from me.

I never heard a word from the Nevada County authorities, I'm sorry to say. All of us who'd been there felt sure someone would call on us to testify at the trial. This one time we'd see justice done to a citizen who victimized cyclists. Alas....

I waited what seemed like a very long time before I called the district attorney at the county seat. He said the county felt it did not have a case against the fellow who'd hit me. He said it was difficult to prove intent, to prove that the guy had *meant* to hit me.

I told the DA that I had never been involved in a thing like this before, that I was not a hysterical, paranoid victim. I told him I rode thousands of miles a year without this sort of incident.

I told him I worked in a bike shop, that I wrote about cycling, that I have good hunches and occasional reliable insights about people. I told him he had a man there in his county who was going to hurt someone, a troubled man. I said that I thought he'd stopped after he hit me because he'd wanted to be caught before he did something bad.

The gentleman from the DA's office said he would take a sincere second look at the case. He carefully wrote down my name, case number, home and work phone numbers—and he never called me back.

Some people told me the thing to do was to sue the guy with the van. Somehow that wasn't how I wanted things to go. I wanted the law to handle it. I wanted the guy prohibited by law from driving so he couldn't hurt you and he couldn't hurt me.

Sure, he was only one of the So Very Many, but he *was* one, and even one was a start. Oh, well, what the hell, eh?

CHRIS

I SAW Chris Carmichael last week for the first time since he got hurt. Chris is one of the boys here in Berkeley, except that he's out of town more than most of us, racing for that convenience-store team you've read about.

When he's home, Carmichael guest-speaks at bike-club meetings. He answers dumb questions from sidewalk strangers as if he found the questions new and interesting. He likes to give cast-offs, like race leader's jerseys he's worn only once, to impoverished juniors.

He speaks softly. He never plays the hero or acts like he's some invulnerable superman.

Carmichael has got to be a better guy than any of the rest of us just to stay even. *He's* a professional bike racer; we are all would-bes and never-wases and could've beens. It would be easy and human of us to find fault with him, to imagine how much neater *we'd* be if *we* rode for 7-Eleven. But we don't. Carmichael is okay.

Last fall, he and a friend drove up to thinly populated northern California to cross-country ski. Carmichael fell while moving slowly and whacked his leg on a rock. He shattered his femur, the bone in his thigh.

While the friend went for help, Carmichael sat on the hillside for three and a half hours trying to remain convinced his femoral artery was not cut. Finally, a helicopter flew him to a hospital.

He lay seven hours in surgery under a waist-down anesthetic, watching the team of doctors at work. A drug they'd given him made him mellow. He watched calmly and listened to the hammering. The doctors had difficulty inserting the long metal rod that now holds Carmichael's femur together. When they eventually succeeded in pounding it up the bone, Carmichael cheered, "*Allez*, doctor," half delirious.

Certain parts of his treatment had to wait. Fatty globules from his bone marrow had been picked up in his bloodstream and deposited in his lungs. Some of that stuff remains there.

His therapy began a few days after the operation. He was asked to get out of his bed and, assisted by orderlies, walk two steps to a wheelchair. Two steps.

Carmichael says he thought that racing the Giro d'Italia was the hardest thing he'd ever have to do—until he got out of that bed.

The doctors told him before the surgery that if the procedure went *really* well, he might walk again. No way, they told him, would he ever again ride a bike. So he couldn't know, at first, what the pain of therapy would earn him. Just to regain his ability to walk wasn't going to cut it.

After a recovery period in the small-town hospital, he was wheeled onto an airplane bound for his family home in Florida, where he could get round-the-clock help. We heard nothing in Berkeley about him for months.

Then in early March, I heard Carmichael'd come back to town, wearing a backpack, flying around on crutches, always at his anaerobic threshold, handicapped but getting fit. Soon I heard he was back on his bike.

I saw him outside our traditional post-ride cafe, drinking coffee with a woman rider. He was just able, he said, to pedal without bouncing in the seat. He hadn't yet gotten his spin back; he had to use sort-of big gears. I noticed his upper leg had an occasionally visible lump in it. I think Carmichael trembled just slightly as we sat in the noontime sun.

He said he'd been a little spooked at first, getting back on the bike.

He said, and his riding friend agreed, that his descending had been jerky at first, but he was gaining smoothness and confidence with the miles.

He said that only the last few days had he been able to follow the pedal with his foot through the whole circle. He told me he was a little afraid to fall. I remembered the Chris Carmichael who could descend faster in the rain than I can in the dry. Here he was having to relearn how to ride downhill.

I thought about what would be demanded of him in the spring, how far he had to go. Most of us would be happy to heal up, ride some miles, maybe do a couple of warm-weather centuries or short road races late in the season. That level of cycling would do fine; it'd be what we'd have to work up to.

Carmichael has to bang elbows with supermen. He has to chase down early breaks towed by locomotives who intend to blow themselves up and quit the race.

He's got to lead out Davis Phinney at sonic-boom speeds in insane packs on shoulder-width streets. He has to ride downhill at speed on roads U.S. bikies wouldn't take their "good" bikes on.

He has done those things and must learn to do them again. He does those things regularly for a living, things I couldn't do even once for a fortune.

Carmichael will be racing by summer. I'm sure there are lots of stories like this one. And probably lots of men and women who've come back from places far worse and done harder things. I just don't know any of them.

I do know Carmichael. So if his team comes to your town, and you get a chance to root for our local boy Chris Carmichael this year, please do not suppress your enthusiasm.

If you are new to the sport and have not selected a favorite rider, you might consider Carmichael. You could do worse. As I've said, I haven't heard all the stories or met all the guys, but in my book, he's a positive hero.

THE ROAD WARRIOR

"NO KIDDING, you're one of those bicyclers? How far do you guys ride? I see bikes, sometimes, hey, way out in the country. Some of those people must really go far.

"You don't ride out in the road, do ya? I ask, 'cause I'll be driving along in my car, you know, and there'll be all these people on bicycles. And they'll be riding out in the road where the cars're supposed to be.

"Lotta times, I'm in a hurry, they block the road. Line of cars has to go slow. It's a big pain.

"Sometimes, if I'm out driving with my girl and we're maybe going out to the country, have a beer at this place we like, we take this road, must be a favorite of all you bicyclers.

"Hey, sometimes I have to pass maybe a dozen of you guys, maybe more. I gotta take a lot of chances over in the oncoming lane, justa get around a bunch of guys in nylon dancing outfits on their damn bicycles.

"You drive a car, doncha? You know what I mean.

"I gotta admit, once in a while I lose my patience. I'm just tryin' to take a little drive with Janey, have a frosty on my day off, and these people have to pick my little road to get their exercise on. I don't know. I guess they don't work or they sit at some desk and talk on

'Hey, these roads weren't built for any damn bicyclers.'

the phone. There they are, every Sunday, gettin' in a guy's way.

"Hey, those roads weren't built for any damn bicyclers. It was my taxes and my registration fees and all that got 'em built and that maintains 'em. Those roads're for cars.

"Messes up the regular flow of things, having a lotta bicyclers on 'em.

"Maybe those people don't drive cars. They don't have the proper respect for the people in the cars, that's for sure. People in cars aren't out there on the road just to be gettin' some goddam fresh air or some exercise.

"They're going someplace. They gotta destination.

"Maybe they're meeting some other people where they're headed. Maybe they're a little late. It's okay to be meeting people, and it's okay to be late and be in a hurry. No harm done, as long as the road's open for the cars.

"I'll be stuck behind a couple of those bicyclers—is that what you call them, bicyclers? —and I start to get a little hot, thinking about how they're taking up as much room in the road as a damn Kenworth or something. Going about 20 mph on a 60 mph road, upsetting everyone up and down the line, not a care in their stupid yuppie heads.

"Hey, after a while, it starts to get me hot, no lie.

"I think to myself, maybe if I don't move over all the way into the other lane when I pass, you know, maybe then they'll realize, if they got the brains God gave a drain pan, that they're in the way.

"They're someplace they don't belong, someplace where they're not wanted, by God. When I pass, I always stay just far enough away so I'm not taking any chances. I only wanna show 'em they can get over, closer to the shoulder, let people get by 'em easier.

"Maybe I'll pull in quick after I pass. Same thing: let's 'em know they're out there with the big boys, where they probably don't wanna be.

"Just a couple weeks ago, I passed these two guys like that. Next thing I know, this striped-ass jerk is yellin' at me, flipping me the bird, for chrissakes. For what? I never hurt him or nothing.

"He wants to get out there on the road on that bike, he's gonna have to act like a grown man, take the good and the bad. That's what it's like, the road.

"I'm watching the guy and, I see he's not gonna understand. I'm not trying to hurt him, just to get him to understand how we feel in the cars. Guy is impeding the flow of traffic for hours, for all I know, spoiling the day's driving for lots of people.

"He thinks he got a right. Yeah. Really thinks the guys in the *cars* are being a pain. Dumbass gives me the finger. Me and Janey. Jesus.

"So I'm looking at the skinny dude in my mirror. There he is, pissed at *me*. Can you believe it? I've been trying to get by him and his buddies all morning, and he's pissed at me. Amazing, huh?

"I give my brakes a little tap, flash the brake lights. He gets freaked and starts screaming again, him and his pal, waving their arms and yelling, and I haven't done a damn thing.

"Hey, I know exactly what I'm doing in my car. Anytime I wanna hurt the guy I can hurt him. I can pick my place.

"But, hey, basically, all I'm doing is trying to show him my viewpoint without us being able to sit down over a couple of beers. Which I wouldn't want to do anyway, 'cause this guy doesn't look like the kinda dude I'd have a beer with.

"And Janey thinks those pants they wear are gross, anyway. You don't wear those things, the shiny ones, do you?

"Then I notice my buddy Charlie is behind the guys, the bicyclers, in his Bronco. He and Suzie are gonna meet me and Janey at the Kountry Klub. Charlie works with me, swing, at Baxter's.

"Charlie, I can see, has been watching what's been happening with these yo-yos, and I know he's pissed. I see Charlie come up close behind those guys. They're talking to each other about how they flipped me the bird and yelled at me and how goddam macho they are. Charlie puts his right front fender under the left-hand guy's elbow, and the guy freaks out.

"I can hear him yell, and I watch him swerve away from Charlie's Bronco and sideswipe his buddy. They get kinda stuck together, and the two of them wiggle around in the road for a couple of seconds. Then they ride off the road together like they're arm in arm down the aisle, for God's sake. Then they fall down.

"Laugh? I laughed so hard, I gotta say, it gave me the giggles like I haven't had since high school. I couldn't stop laughing all afternoon, especially when we got to the Klub, and I look at Charlie, and he's laughing too.

"I think of that guy, that skinny, shiny-assed yuppie in his sun shades, shaking his finger at me like a voodoo curse, gonna ruin my family for generations. And I think of the two of them, the cute couple, wobbling together on them bikes and kicking up dust off the side of the highway.

"Funny? Christ I guess so.

"You don't think it sounds that funny? Well, maybe I'm not telling it right. Maybe you just hadda be there."

THE FREE LUNCH

LET ME tell you a couple of stories; it's what I do, after all. These stories are about testing people's products and how I imagined I could own things I didn't have to pay for, and how I paid for them.

The first story is about a helmet, not a bicycle helmet but a motorcycle one, a clever one that covers the face but features a front half that swivels up so you can talk to people or eat or drink.

One year, I saw lots of those helmets in use at the Coors Classic. They work especially well for bike race support motorcyclists. The races are long and hot. Riders, both bicycle and motorcycle, have to be in the saddle for hours.

That year, my first as a press motorcyclist for the Coors, I had a conventional full-coverage helmet. People were kind enough to hand up waterbottles or Coke cans to my photographer and me on the move during the race, but I could not drink. I lusted for one of the helmets that opened.

Now, in addition to my writing for *Winning* magazine, I write a column for a San Francisco motorcycle newspaper, *CityBike*, that, unlike *Winning*, tests new products. It occurred to me that I might possess one of those new helmets by agreeing to do an evaluation for that newspaper. It was as easily done as said. I rode over to San

Francisco and picked up my new $225 superhelmet free from a cooperating dealer. I was excited.

The thing functioned perfectly during the three road stages I worked. Whenever I wanted, I just opened up my helmet and talked or ate or drank. It was deluxe.

But on the way home from Reno, while my press motorcyclist friends and I burned up Interstate 80, I found that my new helmet's clear plastic shield flew open suddenly whenever I turned my head to look behind, say before a lane change. When we stopped, I checked it out; everything was as it should've been. Curious....

Since then I have fiddled and fiddled with that helmet, to no avail. It persists in flying open when I look back. What the heck, you might say, wear your old helmet. A good idea, but what about the product evaluation? Should I tell my readers the brutal truth? What if my helmet is the only one that does it?

So I called another dealer who sold the helmet. The parts man said, yes, they all do it, at least every one he'd tried. I thanked him and submitted my article with a warning added about the automatic shield.

Then I visited the dealer from whom I'd got the helmet, and guess what? They had sold lots of that model, they said, and had not even one complaint. Probably just mine had that problem.

But the test was already written and rewritten. The truth still eluded me. I felt caught and sorry I'd ever gotten involved. I wished I'd never seen the superhelmet, convenient or not. Which gets us ready for the second story....

One day I happened to answer a call from a very nice fellow who makes a bicycle pedal/shoe system. He, on finding out I worked at a shop that sold his line and that I wrote for *Winning*, offered to send me his products for evaluation.

On my own initiative, I promised to write something for *Winning* about my experience of his equipment.

I figured I could write such a charming, folksy, information-packed article about pedals that Rich Carlson, my editor, would make an exception to *Winning*'s no-tests policy just for me. Naive is not a nearly strong enough word— no, far, far too weak.

Sure enough, two pairs of shoes and a pair of pedals arrived after a couple of weeks, really an expensive package at retail, free for me because I am a shaper of opinion, a mover, a shaker, an idiot.

I screwed the pedals into my cranks and put on the shoes. They fit perfectly. I adjusted the cleats in moments—a snap. I rode in the things for weeks; they were great. In and out effortlessly, never a clumsy moment in an intersection, fumbling for a pedal, taxi honking behind....

I liked everything about this guy's system except the looks of the shoes. The shoes were not good looking. At all. They were *so* not-good-looking that I took continual heat on club rides from my "friends." They did not understand that I was evaluating the system for my readers. They thought, simply, that I had bought and was wearing truly ugly shoes. I kept on wearing them, though, because they worked so well.

I couldn't understand how this nice, bright fellow, who'd gotten it together to develop, fabricate, and market such a terrific system, could have ignored the general vanity of pro-style bikies.

How, I wondered, can he expect to sell these to the kind of riders I know, Euro-style cyclists who want to look as much like Sean Kelly as possible?

So, in a record low moment of judgment I called the gentleman and told him I had written an article about how well his system worked, about how it was a marvel of function. I told him, though, that I thought, and wrote, that the aesthetic aspect of the footwear was negative, saleswise.

I said I had not been anxious to make the call, but I thought I owed it to him to say the difficult thing—that my friends and I found the shoes unattractive. I asked him if I might harmlessly modify my own test shoes to make them more agreeable to the Italophile eye.

The phone began to smoke in my hand. He told me that if I changed the shoes they would no longer be the shoes. He told me that the looks of other products, long established, had changed in response to real innovation. He asked me if I had been put up to making the call or writing the article. He told me I was not being constructive in my criticism.

He stripped from me, in just a few long-distance moments, any taste I had for his merchandise. I scrubbed the article. I put on lesser pedals, lesser shoes. They made me happier.

Clearly, I lack the hide for the product-evaluation thicket. I'm glad I've found a niche in bicycle writing that does not require me to make subtle judgments that might affect someone's living. I've seen how folks' cordiality can leak away if they suspect that the slightest negative reference to their product might get into print.

I've seen how hard the truth can be to get at. I think I'll let the racers test the stuff. I'll write about the sport.

The two experiences I've described have given me a new respect for writers who can conclude that "they all do it" from the evidence of one or two examples and who can cope with loud, unhappy voices on the phone. Let those guys take the heat. Me, I'm gonna stay way out of the kitchen.

FRANGIBLE
FRAMESETS

"HELLO, FRANGIBLE Framesets. This is Falconer Frangible. How may we help you?"

"Oh, hi. I'm calling from Fallen Ego, Tennessee. I think I may be ready for a custom frameset. Would you mind if I asked you a few questions?"

"Not at all. We feel, at Frangible, that the more our customers know about us and about our products—fast frames for fastidious frame buyers—the more readily they will call on us when the buying bug eventually bites."

"Well, I'm not a bicycle racer, but I like to ride around our area with my friends. It's hilly west of here and mostly flat to the east. We generally ride weekends and a couple nights a week after work. Do I need a chain-hanger braze-on? I should tell you I use deep-drop handlebars. I carry one waterbottle and two pumps. And you should know I'm into short-reach brakesets, totally, as was my father before me."

"I see. Do you have our full-color Frangible Frameset folder? Perhaps, if you study it carefully, it will help you answer some of your questions."

"Why, no, I don't. I just saw your ad in *Bicycle Fancier* magazine. I thought I'd give you a call. We have a WATS line here at work. I'm on a break, so there's no hurry. If you could clear up a problem or two while I have you on the phone...."

"Sure. Just let me turn off this torch. Our customers are more than just frame sizes to us here at Frangible, the Firmly Flexible Frameset for Frankly Fussy Aficionados. Fire away."

"Gee, thanks. Tell me, how do you feel about composites? I mean, I know you have a vested interest in steel, but don't you think steel is, well, yesterday's technology? If I stand up when I climb, will a Frangible frame flex? Will the gears shift by themselves? Will the chain come off? What if I wax it? How many frames have you made? How many have broken? Do folks riding Frangible Frames fall frequently? Are Frangibles fast? Have they been evaluated in *Bicycle Science* magazine? Do I really need a custom frame, or should I just buy my buddy's baby-blue Bowlachili? It has a bent fork."

"First of all, let me assure you that we at Frangible are absolutely, positively, unequivocally certain that steel is still the foremost material for frameset fabrication."

"But isn't it heavy?"

"More or less. But Frangible Framesets have a feel, a fineness, a flowing oneness with the road. They caress the tarmac with an almost sensual sureness, a supple rigidity. Excuse me, are you over 18? Oh, good. We think that the ineffable Frangible feeling principally depends on the flexible firmness of steel."

"Sounds terrific, but are your frames straight? I've heard some builders hardly even check to see if their tips are parallel."

"Straight? Straight? Why, our framesets are so forcefully straight we've had to curtail sales in certain neighborhoods in San Francisco and Atlanta for fear of rejection. Our alignments are done on a flat table—so flat that other builders send their tables here to measure just how crooked they are. Fishhooks on our premises will straighten themselves out, untouched, in seconds. Roads in our area never bend."

"How do I go about getting sized?"

"Excellent question. Generally, we work from full-length skeletal x-rays. We have an in-house sports physician on our team here at Frangible. He examines each prospective owner's bone structure and factors in such aspects as musculature and riding habits, typical gear selection, intended frame use, geographic area, and barometric pressure. All in an exhaustive effort to extrapolate the perfect, ideal, and totally correct frame configuration for you and you alone. Naturally, that process can take some time, but finicky Frangible riders appreciate our dedication. We usually correspond by registered mail in cases of far-off applicants like yourself. I would allow about $25 for postage during the fitting procedure and $50, more or less, for the frontal and lateral x-rays. It'll be worth it. We believe a properly sized bicycle has a classical symmetry, a recognizable rightness, that none but a Frangible owner can count on."

"Fascinating. Do you do your own paint work?"

"Frangible finishes are justifiably famous. First the frameset is filed, a process that can take our team of four first-class filers 16 to 18 hours. Then it is dipped for several days in an anticorrosive to preserve it for the quality-minded cyclist post-millennium. Only then is it finished in the most painstakingly patient process, using ultra-expensive materials. This consumes so much time that work on an individual frame may be handed down from father to son. After the optional, and beautiful, Frangible transfers are applied, we tenderly spray 12 coats of clear sealer under surgically sterile conditions, virtually guaranteeing several decades of satisfaction with the finish. We are proud of our craftsmanship here at Frangible. You yourself can experience that same pride in the form of your own, personal, one-of-a-kind frameset, signed by myself after a meticulous preshipment inspection. Signed for all your admiring friends to see—*Falconer Frangible.*"

"Gosh, Mr. Frangible...."

"Call me Falconer, please."

"Oh, sure, uh, Falconer. You know, I've called a framebuilder every day on my break for almost three weeks now. You are by far the most confidence-inspiring. You've got me really interested. If I decided to begin the Frangible Frameset selection process, how long would it be before I had my frame in my hands?"

"You're in Tennessee, you said? Let me see. I could have one there for you UPS in eight or nine days, less if we ship Blue Label. Even sooner, if you can get into metallic green. Can you ride a 25½? Want a headset? VISA or MasterCard?"

177

THE OLD FARTS RIDE

THIS MORNING I rode the San Francisco area Old Farts Ride. Mostly, the Old Farts guys raced in the '60s. Some of them still look fit and trim, evidently riding several times a week. A few don't ride as often as they'd like. One or two get out more often than they'd lead you to believe.

We had a five-time Nevada City winner there, Bob Parsons, and a sixth-place finisher at the Montreal Olympics, George Mount. Because it was a northern California crowd, it was mostly old roadies, plus a few criterium riders and a trackie or two.

Natural-fiber clothing abounded. Lots of riders wore tights and arm-warmers well into the warmth of the day. Two fellows mourned the losses to shrinkage of their old, original Berkeley Wheelmen (now defunct) jerseys.

Those hallowed garments had pointed collars like dress shirts, buttons where jerseys now have zippers, and pockets across the chests. They were made from 100-percent wool; anything else was unthinkable. Nowadays, though, most Old Farts wear helmets and Lycra—at least they did this morning. Several guys used, or talked of using, heart-rate monitors.

Kim Bruseth showed up on his ancient mostly-Campy brown

Bianchi, still equipped with TA cranks and Universal centerpull brakes. He's been riding that old bike all these years. Most of the fellows had updated their equipment, though. I saw a good-looking orange Bruce Gordon, two Vituses, and a modern Belgian cobblestone bike.

I saw a few indexed-shifting setups, a couple sets of clipless pedals, and some of those new tires that don't have to be glued to the rim.

All the men, and the only woman on the ride, Old Fart Vance Vaughn's friend Elaine Mariolle, not an old-timer herself, could ride their bikes well. So well that I found myself moving backwards in the group on descents. That is not totally uncommon, however. My downhill ability may be less impressive, even, than my sprint.

I thought it curious that, in this group of Europhile California cycling "pioneers," not one voice was accented. All those guys are probably (at least) second-generation Americans. I suspect that might not be the case in the Midwest or East. Feel free to correct me if I'm wrong.

Some of the conversations sounded like those you might hear on young-guy rides. Some others, I thought, showed a different perspective. I heard three guys say they agreed that much of cycling history has been lost. Magic names like Coppi, Anquetil, and Nencini, greats from pre-Merckx days, are nearly forgotten.

Someone remarked that if it were not for Owen Mulholland, who tends the flame, many faithful bicycle-magazine readers could forget that there was bike racing before Andy Hampsten was born.

George Mount said that, in Italy, such lore is not neglected, but continually renewed. Magazines print achievement comparisons between some current superstar and, say, Fausto Coppi. Coppi, Mount said, inevitably emerges the greater rider. Ah, *Italia....*

Al Muller told me he rides after work with three younger guys. Muller, 59, has a sit-down-and-spin riding style. He says he can spin uphill with his training partners just fine. But if his friends try to climb in *his* choice of gear, they can't do it; they have to slow down.

Parsons, in his early 40s, rides in Santa Cruz with the boys. He says he has to use a bigger gear than the kids do, to hang in on the shorter hills. I asked him if he uses the same gear the young guys do on long hills. He said he never has the chance to find out. They just ride away, he told me. Sigh....

The men talked enthusiastically about food. Some of them had indeeed put on a pound or two over the years. Nevertheless, they managed to haul it all up and over the East Bay hills, perhaps just to qualify for the post-ride barbecue and beer.

As I looked around at these genuine veterans gathered in Steve Yee's back yard, I wondered how many times their lives must have seemed to conspire against their riding; how often jobs or mates or injuries or bad luck might have tried to pry them off their bikes. Indeed, some of them had spent years off, or barely on, the bike, but they had eventually returned to the sport.

One or two of them were big winners in their day: George Mount was the first U.S. finisher at the Giro; Bob Parsons held the deed to Nevada City for half a decade. Most of the others were just good bike riders, about like you and me. They are all good guys; I can vouch for that. I rode with 'em this morning and, as folks to ride and chat with, they'll be hard to beat.

It gave me a good feeling, being involved in a sport like ours, a sport that can attract and keep on attracting such people as these. I only got to spend the one morning getting to know them, putting faces with names I'd heard for years. Doesn't take long, though, when you meet these NorCal bikie legends, to get the feeling they're okay.

Even though a few ride those new-fangled pedals, there's nothing trendy about their attitude toward cycling. No yuppie "no-pain, no-gain" intensity. No pretense that expensive equipment equals commitment or speed. And no special treatment for today's hero, who'll be an Old Fart soon enough anyway.

These men can remember when there was nothing trendy about cycling, when people who persevered at it had to be pretty dedicated.

Nowadays, our sport is so hot it attracts short-termers like a Motel 6. It took a 50-mile morning with guys like those Old Farts to remind me that no one loves cycling like the men and women who're in it for the long ride.

SHOPS LIKE BOB'S

WHEN I started writing my column for *Winning* magazine, "The Bike Shop" described the activity around a small bicycle store. Bob, the owner, represents an idealized bike shop proprietor. Bob is a rider and a friend of riders. He's a source of equipment, encouragement, and help to a community of cyclists.

Lots of readers liked those stories—liked them better, for all I know, than the ones I write now. People still tell me how much they liked this or that story about Bob and the characters around his store. More than a few have tried to pin an identity on Bob. He's so admirable I hope any shop owner would be flattered to be thought the "real" Bob. I know for sure Bob's a better retail guy than I am, though I try.

Bob's store is my idea of the kind of place I'd shop in. I'd like to stop by and purchase my sew-ups and glue from ol' Bob. I'd say hi to the promising woman racer working the counter. I'd pat Bob's latest junior hotshot on the shoulder.

Bob would take time to listen to me. He'd try to understand my situation or problem, if I had one. There'd be person-to-person contact. I'd pay a fair price for what I needed. I'd leave thinking: "What a super guy." Maybe I'd feel a little super, myself, because of

Bob's treating me the way he would. Bob makes you feel like that. Super.

Hey, I could go anywhere and buy tires and glue. Probably there's someplace I could get them for less money. Me, though, I'd get them from Bob. I like him, and I think he cares about me over and above me-as-a-customer. He cares about bike riding and about bike riders.

Bike riding and bike riders—Bob's got it right. Those are the things in our sport that matter. Sadly, they are things that, in my retail bike shop jobs, I have almost never been asked about, almost never encouraged to talk about. All I get to talk about is bikes. Hardware. Consumer goods. *Blech.*

I don't think a bike shop should be like a department store, not even a nice, helpful department store. A bike shop should be the kind of place, ideally, where you might go even if you don't need anything. A place where you'd feel part of that community of cyclists, bonded to that community irrespective of what brand of bike you ride or what flashy pro jersey you wear.

Bike riding is not about consuming. You can't get fit buying things. Try it. No matter how many "things" you buy, the hills will be steep.

Bike shops that are mostly just places to buy things thrive and will thrive, whether I write this piece or not. Our little underground sport has gotten bigtime, merchandising-wise. Huge temples of label-worship have risen in the west. All are cleverly, beautifully designed and amazing to see.

Most of these stores employ real bike riders/enthusiasts as sales people. The stores carry, say, 10 lines of top Italian professional bicycles. Tell me what a real bike rider/enthusiast finds to say about which $1,850 Italian handmade masterpiece you should buy. Which of the 100 jerseys in stock in your size should you wear? Which high-tech pedal system? Which winter trainer? *Gulp.*

I still remember the thrill of buying my first classy Italian part: the beige box, the rainbow stripes. Bike shop self-service is convenient, I suppose, but where's the excitement in reaching into a bin and selecting the C-Record derailleur that'll be yours from 75 more just like it?

In Italy, I'm told, in most shops, the customer asks for a part and the

counterperson goes in the back and gets it. The shop owner, like Bob, serves as the local coach, sponsor, and, probably, framebuilder.

Clearly, things are done differently here. We love our options, love to shop. We pore over technical articles deciding where to place our "disposable" incomes. But do all the reams and reams of obvious and subtle hype enable you to make informed decisions? Tell me, then, which lightweight, narrow, folding high-pressure clincher should I buy? Which one's best? Should I ask the busy counterperson who has 15 varieties in stock and no time to ride? How can he or she know? Who do you call?

I don't believe this piece is just a nostalgic plea for simpler times. There are shops like Bob's all over the country, even now. Perhaps they're not as perfect as Bob's has appeared to be, but Bob has free rent and suffers retail stress for only 1,000 words every few months.

When I started riding, I was lucky. I lived near a bike store where a guy worked who had seen Eddy Merckx race at his brutal best. That same guy remembered drinking from alloy water bottles with cork stoppers. He knew for certain that Alfredo Binda was, at one time, more than a name on a toestrap.

I hope there's a shop like that and a person like that very near you.

Author MAYNARD HERSHON lives near San Francisco with his wife, Shelly Glasgow. He rides bicycles and motorcycles and writes about both experiences. Born and raised in the midwest, he moved west in the mid-60s to California, where, he says, he is dodging adulthood to this day. Hershon started cycling in 1975, and in 1983 began writing "The Bike Shop" column in *Winning* magazine. Most of the stories in this book first appeared in that column.

Illustrator JEF MALLETT, a former licensed bicycle racer, lives in Lansing, MI, where he is art director for Booth Newspapers.